SANCTUARY

THE SOLDIER: BOOK TWO

W.J. LUNDY

COPYRIGHT

Whiskey Tango Foxtrot

SANCTUARY
The Soldier: Book 2
By W. J. Lundy

CHAPTER ONE

DAY OF INFECTION, PLUS EIGHTEEN

North of Hayslette, Virginia

Rounds punched into the Sheetrock overhead, the space filled with dust and rifle smoke. Gyles rolled away from the impacts, bits of plaster biting at his face. He crawled behind the meat counter to his rear. A bright flash of light and an explosion from the front of the building washed out his night vision. He shoved the now useless NVG (Night Vision Goggles) up and away from his eyes then pressed his back to the wall. He could sense a soldier directly to his right, another to his left. Even though pitch-black, he knew they were there. He could hear their heavy breathing, the clattering of their equipment. Gyles grabbed for the Motorola radio microphone hanging off his right shoulder.

"Cease fire, cease fire! You're hitting us in the crossfire, dammit!"

The gunfire continued at a frantic pace. More incoming rounds zipped overhead, the telltale buzzing of near misses smacking the meat counter. Glass and metal exploded and popped as it was riddled with rounds. He rolled back to the ground, pressed against the gritty tile floor, trying to make himself small while rounds pinged and smacked all around him. The howls of the Primals filled every break in the gunfire. He reached for the radio again, but before he could speak, the building went silent.

A weak voice broke the silence. "I'm hit."

Another call, this time from his left. "Medic! I need a medic."

Gyles moved to a knee and leaned forward, peering over the meat case to his front. Staring into the darkness, he dropped his night vision goggles back over his eyes. In the smoke and dust, it was nearly impossible to see. He picked up on muffled voices of the squad to his front. He flipped on the infrared headlight, illuminating the space in artificial light that could only be seen in his goggles. His men appeared in tones of green and black.

What only minutes before looked like a clear, vacant, grocery store—a place with fully stocked shelves—was now a scene of carnage. The infected lay dead across the floors, shelves of goods destroyed from automatic weapons fire. Rifle smoke and the stench of burnt gun oil filled the air. At the far end of the store, he could see the sparkle of Second Squad's infrared headlights, the green lasers from their rifles cutting through the smoke, and the twinkle of the IR strobes off their equipment.

They had attempted to secure the large grocery store. Recon elements moved in first, using cameras and surveillance drones, then Second and Third Squads moved through the main entrance as Gyles took up the rest of the platoon and cut through the loading dock doors. The plan was to secure and seal the building at both ends. With all of their heavy weapons at the front, they hoped to be attacked there. Then Gyles would use his team to bring the goods out through the docks to be loaded onto trucks, which would be arriving as soon as they entered and cleared the structure. They ran this operation plenty of times and never had a problem until today.

They covered every approach, and the recon elements said the store was empty. Gyles moved his team up, breached the warehouse doors, and then something had gone horribly wrong.

He reached back to the radio. "Reaper One, this is Five; what the hell is going on over there?"

"Five, this is One. We had heavy contacts pour in through a manager's office. We missed it on the recon; they got between us. Sorry 'bout the crossfire."

Gyles shook his head and sighed. "Get security set up, lock this place down—no more surprises. The trucks are on station and we're beginning the load out. I want to be on the road ASAP."

"Roger that, we're on it."

Gyles clenched his jaw and looked to a soldier

kneeling beside him. Sergeant Alvarez, a former Georgia National Guardsmen assigned to his new platoon of Army veterans. The man was strong and reliable and had quickly made himself valuable to the team. He was fast to rally the troops and possessed a natural ability to remain calm under fire. Gyles was surprised at how Alvarez always managed to know the pulse of the platoon, like it was a living and breathing creature. If something was amiss with the men, Alvarez knew it.

"How we looking?" Gyles whispered.

"Kipperson took a hit," Alvarez said, turning away. He flipped up his NODS and used the sleeve of his forearm to wipe away sweat.

Gyles knew the kid, but just barely. Kipperson was a private, an active duty wrench-turner they'd recovered from a stranded convoy three days earlier. He was a mechanic by trade, but with the state of everything, every man was now a shooter as far as Gyles was concerned. Many of the recent adds to the Reaper Platoon had come to him that way.

Men he didn't know, skills as diverse as the passengers on a New York City subway. As the senior Army member of the camp, Gyles was made the impromptu leader of all the Army elements. And playing second fiddle to the Marines that ran the camp, the Reapers found themselves out running salvage missions as the Marines defended the camp and looked for survivors. Even with every resource in the field, the camp was on life support. They were day-to-day on food, and the numbers of infected outside the gates doubled daily. That meant every available soldier moved out on every mission; they needed everything they had to keep the survivors fed.

Gyles grimaced and looked back at his squad leader. "The mechanic. How is he?"

The junior sergeant pursed his lips and shook his head. In the pixilated view of the night vision goggles, Gyles knew he'd lost a man.

"He bled out, Sergeant, hit bad." Alvarez paused and let out a deep breath. "Hell, even a medevac and level one trauma center wouldn't have made a difference for him. What the hell happened, boss? Thought this place was empty."

Gyles frowned and slowly dipped his chin in understanding. There were no EVACs here, no medical helicopters or ambulances to bail them out if they got into trouble. Only two weeks into the end of the world and the support model had gone to shit. With the camp being the only known forces in the region, the Reapers were on their own if they got their asses caught in a sling. There was no backup, no quick reaction force to come to the rescue in Primal country. That was just how it worked now, and his men had come to accept it.

"I don't know, Alvarez." He exhaled loudly and ordered, "Leave two men to recover his body then take the rest of the squad into the structure. We need to start loading the trucks with anything in here still worth salvaging."

"We'll get it done, Sergeant," the man said, turning back toward the rest of the unit, the men still spread out along the back wall of the market.

Gyles stood and walked away from the others, considering the vastness of the store to his front. There was everything in here... food, hardware, clothing, even auto parts. He wished he had the trucks to really empty the place out, but food was priority.

Chem lights were snapped and tossed into the aisles of the market. Soft, green light glowed around them, lighting the space and exposing the carnage. Gyles pushed his night vision device up again and saw soldiers running down aisles with large bags, deploying them at scattered intervals, as others began stuffing them full of dry goods. He turned at the sounds of squeaking wheels and saw a pair of soldiers pushing rows of shopping carts.

Other men hastily filled the metal baskets-on-wheels with canned goods then looped back, running them to the trucks. It was like that in Primal country. Things might be quiet now, but they could change in an instant. Every minute outside the walls was a gamble. Gyles rubbed the back of his neck and looked toward the wall, where two of his men were bagging the body of Private Kipperson.

"Groceries for a life," he whispered to himself. "How long can we keep this up?"

"What was that, G-Man?"

Gyles turned and saw Weaver beside him. "Sorry about the friendly fire, boss. They were on us like stink on shit. If we hadn't let loose when we did—well, they would have eaten our asses for sure." Weaver looked beyond his platoon sergeant to the soldiers bagging the body. "Oh shit. I didn't know."

"This is on me," Gyles said, looking away. "I shouldn't have divided the platoon. Should have kept us together and cleared the store front to back." He turned and looked back at Weaver. "You said they came in from a manager's office. How the fuck did the recon team not notice them on the sweep?"

Weaver dipped his chin and pointed his flashlight to the west side of the building. "Yeah, over there behind the Home and Garden area... pair of hidden doors. Recon boys are already on it. They said it looks like an old stock room converted to admin use. They just missed it; the door didn't stand out to them. And whoever hid there post fall tried to disguise the opening. The noise breaching the warehouse doors must have woke up the Stalkers."

"Stalkers?" Gyles asked.

Weaver grunted. "It's what the recon troops have taken to calling the sneaky ones. The little bastards that lay in wait. Guess they've had some run-ins."

"Primals that ambush—how much worse can it get?" Gyles shook his head and stepped off. "Never mind, let's go check it out."

They walked past the soldiers, who were moving both ways in pairs, running full carts out to the large trucks while others returned with empty ones. Nearing the aisles, Gyles could see that the damage to the stock

7

wasn't as bad as he'd first expected. There were still plenty of undamaged canned items and entire shelves of dry goods.

"This is a good take—a lot more in here than I expected to find," Weaver said, observing the teams.

Gyles nodded. "Yeah, but even with all this... what is it? Two, maybe three days of food? By the time we split it between the barracks and the survivor camp, we're still all going to be losing some weight."

"Hey, boss, if a day's work buys us three days on the right side of the dirt, that's a win in my book." Weaver lowered his voice and moved closer. "Say, you heard any news from DC? Someone else has got to be out there. How long you think we have to hold before the rest of the division rolls in and relieves us?"

Gyles shook his head and moved past the men, not interrupting their progress. "Nothing. I agree someone has to be there. We didn't do anything special, and we made it this far." He followed a path of dead Primal bodies through the store and into the home and garden area. It was the only place he saw any signs of looting. A glass case in the sporting goods corner was smashed. Empty ammo boxes and trigger locks lay on the floor.

Gyles pointed at the mess. "Someone got them-selves strapped."

"You think they are in here?" Weaver said.

Gyles shook his head. "Hope not. If they are, they've turned."

Ahead of them came muffled voices and flashes of light; Weaver's men had already secured the office area. Gyles moved to a pair of free-swinging doors and pushed them open, stepping inside. The space had a foul musty odor, like unwashed bodies and human waste. The office area that once held cubicles and desks had been dismantled and stacked like firewood. The remnants of office furniture piled high barricaded a rear exit door on the back wall. The center of the floor, where the desks had been, was now covered with tents and sleeping bags. The large space had been converted to a full-on campsite. The only thing remaining in place was a large wooden conference table covered with camp stoves and dishes. Cases of canned goods were stacked up against a near wall.

Gyles pointed at the stockpile. "Make sure someone gets that stuff, can't afford to leave anything behind."

Weaver nodded and looked at the tents, pointing his rifle barrel at the huddle of them. "They had it pretty good in here. Loads of food and water, walls on all sides. Hell, better than the base camp even." Weaver nodded and turned in a 360, taking in a full view. "This place was locked down. Doors at both ends of the market were secure... whatever got them didn't break in. They let it in."

Gyles moved toward a body and knelt over it. The middle-aged man wore denim pants and a Realtree camo T-shirt. His head was twisted back with the mouth wide open, his right hand still clutching a Mossberg shotgun. Expended shell casings littered the floor between the dead man's boots. The body had been ravaged, a chunk of the throat missing. Gyles reached for a jacket near the body and placed it over the man's head. "Someone got inside. They got close, or the fighting would have been near the entrance or outside. We didn't find any dead out there."

Weaver turned on his own flashlight and lifted back a flap on one of the larger tents. He flinched then stepped back, shaking his head. "More of the dead in there."

Gyles moved closer. The tent floor was covered with bloody bandages, gauze, and bodies in the same mangled state. He rubbed his temples. "Someone let an infected in; they tried to patch him or her up and they turned, most likely at night. This fella was probably on watch. He did what he could, but it wasn't enough. Once he fell, it was just a matter of time." He sighed and looked down at a child's body. "Lots of folks bit— probably hid all over the store, waited until the infections took hold, and they turned one by one. Why do they still take in the injured?"

Weaver shrugged. "The only cure is a bullet. People know it, but they just can't do it when it's their own family and friends."

Frowning, Gyles said, "This thing just doesn't stop killing." He looked to a pair of soldiers patrolling the space then stared at the scene a final time, imagining what horrors must have taken place. He spotted a child's shoe, and his eyes fixed on it. Suddenly feeling ill, he called it. "Bag up anything useful and get the hell out of here. We egress in ten mikes." He turned to Weaver. "Come on, I need some air."

The pair moved through the market and exited the back doors, onto the loading docks, where the trucks were nearly filled. They continued down the steps to a back lot where men stood watch. The men of the recon team were across the street, rifles up, watching a faraway intersection. The surrounding city was silent, not a single vehicle on the road, no movement on the distant sidewalks. The place was a literal ghost town. A young soldier quickly ran from the recon team across the street, stopping just short of Gyles's side, and made a report.

"So—nothing then? No contact?" Gyles asked, clarifying. "Where the hell is everyone?"

"No, Sergeant, even when the shooting started, it stayed quiet out here. But the recon team found this on the corner," the man said, holding a scrap of white cardboard. Its blue ink had run, and the paper was warped from the rain. He handed it to Gyles. "It was stuck to a telephone pole."

Survivors—come to the church, all are welcome.

Gyles stared at the words, then turned and passed the strip of cardboard to Weaver. "What do you make of it?"

Weaver shrugged and passed the paper back. "Doesn't matter what we think; it's not our mission. We salvage the market and RTB. We got enough mouths to feed."

"We just return to base, even though there could be people out there?"

Laughing, Weaver shook his head side to side. "That's not even what that note says. It could mean anything. And you were the one just bitching about the supply situation. Three days, right?"

"Really?" Gyles grunted and shook his head, ignoring the comment about mouths to feed. "It says *survivors*. How could that mean anything else?"

"Don't mean they are asking for help," Weaver said again. "Sounds to me like they are asking folks to join them."

Gyles nodded and looked back to the young soldier. "You heard anything from Alamo?"

The man shook his head. "No, Sergeant, the radios are still hacked. Just clicks and static. Only the small Motorolas at short range seem to avoid whatever it is jamming us up."

Gyles rubbed the stubble on his chin and looked at the note a bit longer before folding the strip of cardboard and stuffing it into a cargo pocket on his trousers. "Yeah, you're right, Weaver." He turned and looked back as his men exited the market, securing the doors behind them. He could tell by the way they were grouping up that the trucks were loaded, and they were ready to go. "Mission priority is getting this food back to Camp Alamo."

He looked out toward the city streets then back to the group surrounding him. He faced Weaver and said, "Get the convoy back to base. I'm taking a truck and four men. I want to head toward town and see if I can find this church."

"Come on, bro, you can't be serious," Weaver said, moving closer.

"I'm not leaving anyone out there if we can help it," Gyles said. "Not again."

Weaver sighed and put his hand on Gyles's shoulder. "G-man, what happened at the armory wasn't your fault."

Gyles pulled away and hardened his jaw. "Sergeant, get these supplies back to Alamo."

CHAPTER TWO

DAY OF INFECTION, PLUS EIGHTEEN

Camp Alamo, Near Hayslette, Virginia

L uke moved down the long, narrow hallway and into the communal area of the machine works factory, a large open bay filled with cots and tarps. At one end was a spacious kitchen area, where makeshift tables were organized in a similar fashion to a high school cafeteria. The family housing section was a converted factory floor with entrances on each end. There were two of them, to be exact—housing areas Alpha and Bravo, both filled to double the capacity of what was originally estimated.

Above their heads, stretching the perimeter of the building and crisscrossing the floor, were steel catwalks patrolled by Marines. Places normally walked by plant electricians and foremen were now the stomping grounds of heavily armed security forces.

On the factory floor, keeping order was the responsibility of civilian law enforcement—made of remnants of state and county police officers and another dozen former cops. Being a sheriff's deputy put him into the rotation to make the daily presence patrols down in the survivors' camp. His hand drifted to his empty holster. Nobody on the floor was allowed firearms, including the law enforcement. All weapons were checked at the main entrance. All he had was a collapsible baton which he wore on his duty belt next to an empty pepper spray pouch.

He didn't like being disarmed in here, but he understood it. With the infection just outside the factory walls, paranoia and fear were high, and everyone was on edge. Even though everybody was given a rigorous exam for infection before being allowed inside, mistakes still happened, and the survivors here had reasons to be afraid. The last thing they needed was for a shootout to occur over a suspected outbreak. It had happened before, with several killed, and the Colonel was adamant that it would not happen again. Luke moved deeper into the family areas and past children playing, then beyond a cluster of civilians being led in prayer by a white-bearded priest. Along a wall, a pair of men in heavy coats skinned a deer as a couple women stretched meat from a previous kill over a low fire for smoking.

Most men were confined to the buildings of Camp Alamo, but the Colonel had made exceptions for some of the hunters and anglers who'd proven themselves able to bring home game. They would go out with the patrols and be dropped near hunting grounds to be retrieved on the return trips. Stopping and watching the men work, Luke could see they must have had a good hunt. One of the hunters turned to see him looking. The man nodded and held up a hunk of venison. Luke smiled and waved the man off. The man returned the smile and quickly turned back to the carcass he was processing.

Luke passed the hunters and leaned against the wall near the prayer circle. Annoyed glances caught his eye from the parishioners, but they weren't looking at him. Their grievances were from the shouts of laughter coming from behind a long blue tarp that had been hung to cordon off a corner of the factory floor. An old woman with pulled-back grey hair locked eyes with him then turned her head toward the tarps. She quickly lowered her gaze before Luke could speak. The woman was afraid to make a report, but her eyes told him everything he needed to know.

Luke had been a cop long enough to know the signs of an intimidated population, and this camp was quickly becoming one. Even though closely guarded by the military and patrolled by police, the floor-dwelling community had become its own subculture. The population had divided, with elements taking charge, even if not officially. He shook his head, looking at the people gathered in protective circles. It reminded him of a prison; there was no freedom here. This was no way to live. These people wouldn't last here—if the Primals outside didn't get them, they would devour themselves inside.

He put his hands on his hips and looked at the long blue tarp hung from the bottoms of the catwalk above. He moved beyond the gathered congregation and headed toward the screened off area. The tarp was new, but he knew from previous walks through here, that there was a water tap and restrooms on the far side. As the only water supply for the entire factory floor, there had always been lines here on his previous visits. Now the corner was quiet, and he intended to find out why.

Stepping closer, he stood outside the tarp and listened to the laughter on the other side. He clenched his jaw and pulled back a cut on the tarp and stepped through. Inside, he found a trio of rough men standing over the water point. Behind them was a large tap with a length of rubber hose and a deep stainless-steel basin. They were laughing at a young girl wearing a small backpack. She was tall but frail, maybe seventeen; it was hard to judge because of her thin stature. Luke moved in stealthily, his presence not known to the trio. The girl held a crumpled gallon water jug. She was asking for it to be filled as the men toyed with her.

"What you got in trade, girl?" a gangly man in a sleeveless flannel shirt asked. As he spoke, his voice cracked with laughter. "You know, this water ain't cheap."

Luke could tell by his posture that he was the gang leader. He spoke not with authority, but infliction in his voice that begged for attention and laughs from the others in his mob.

A second, heavyset, squat man snatched the jug from the girl in a quick motion, nearly knocking her to the floor as she flinched away. A third, square-chested man pushed his shoulders out and howled with laughter. "Shit, girl, now you ain't even got a jug to carry it. How you fixin' to buy a jug to hold all that water?" He howled again. "This day just getting expensive for you, ain't it?"

The girl stepped away and shook her head. "Please —I just need the water."

The gangly leader laughed again. "Like we said, how you fixin' to pay for it?"

Luke had heard enough; he stepped forward, ensuring to stomp his boot heels as he moved into the space. Gangly took his eyes off the girl and looked back at him, his face registering surprise to find him already inside their makeshift shelter.

The man's eyes shifted left to right, trying to determine if the lawman was alone. "Aww hell, look at this, boys. It's Johnny Law," he said with the others choking back laughs and giggles. "What can we do ya for, Sheriff? You looking for water? You know the law always drinks for free at our tap."

Luke took a few steps closer, positioning himself tactically, stopping just over the girl's left shoulder. He crossed his hands in front of himself and glanced at the girl, who looked back at him with desperate eyes. He exhaled softly and shook his head. "So, what—you chuckle monkeys just decided this is your tap now? That what's going on here? I don't remember water rights being a thing in this camp."

Gangly smiled with crooked teeth. "Oh no, it ain't nothing like that. Yeah, we just guarding it, you know, just to make sure everyone is sharing and whatnot. We don't want just a couple folks hogging all the water."

Luke tucked his upper lip and nodded thought-fully. "Didn't realize that had become a problem."

"Oh, it ain't; not yet," Gangly said. "Mostly because we been keeping things orderly and all that."

"So, you are filling the girl's jug then?" Luke asked. "You know, with the way you all are just helping out."

The big barrel-chested man took a step toward Luke, smiling out of the side of a clenched mouth. "Heck, we wanted to, but turns out the girl ain't got no jug. We was in the middle of bartering when you interrupted."

This time, it was Luke who smiled. He looked toward the girl. "Young lady, is that your jug?"

She went to speak, but before she did, her jaw began to tremble and she shook her head no. Luke nodded. "I see." He pointed to the jug in the squat man's hands. "How about you all give her that one then. You don't need it, do you? You seem to have plen-ty," Luke said, pointing to a pile of empty water jugs stacked behind the trio.

Squatty laughed. "Nope, she can't have this one here—it's a family heirloom," he said, causing the other two to burst into raucous laughter. "And those there have all been reserved for others. We got them on hold for preferred clients."

Luke sighed and rolled his shoulders. "I seriously can't believe you are willing to take an ass beating over a faded and half-crushed empty milk jug."

"Da hell did you say to me, boy?" the barrel-chested man snarled, pushing his biceps out and taking another step forward. "I wouldn't go getting all uppity in this camp just cause you're wearing a badge. Shit ain't the same as it was a month ago, you know."

Luke held his smile on the man, his expression hardly changing. "I said fill the girl's jug and let her be. Do that, and you can sleep with all of your teeth tonight." Luke paused and squinted at the man's jaw. "Well, at least with the few rotten teeth you have left, you greasy, pork chop-looking sack of turds."

Without another word, the barrel-chested man charged forward. Luke had anticipated the aggressive move and stepped quickly to the side. He kicked out with the toe of his boot, catching the man's ankle and tripping him. The man tumbled forward, into the concrete floor. Luke canted his body and bent his knees. Just as the man turned and looked up at him, Luke delivered a swift, but controlled kick to his face, the steel toe of his boot landing with a sickening crack.

Luke pivoted back and faced off the two remaining men. Squatty stepped backward, while Gangly glared at him with his jaw locked. The presumed leader tried to appear threatening, but it was obvious the tall man was a coward and not a fighter. Luke looked back down at the grounded man, who was attempting to rise with his eyes spinning in his head. He grunted then dropped flat to his back, unconscious. The trio's muscle lay on the floor, bleeding from his mouth.

Luke pointed a finger at Squatty. "The jug, fill it."

Squatty nodded and stretched out his arm to hand it over.

"No, you fill it first," Luke said. "And say one more word, and I'll drop you like your sack-of-shit friend."

The man gritted his teeth and dropped the jug. He shook his head and stepped back, pulling a long-bladed knife from his back.

"Ahh, look at that. The pig has teeth after all," Luke said. He looked to Gangly. "What about you? You got balls too, or are you going to let your fat girl-friend do your fighting?"

Gangly snarled yellow teeth and clenched his fists. "Why, you son of a bitch. You'll regret this."

Luke grinned, pulling the collapsible baton from the back of his duty belt. He snapped it to its full length. "How 'bout we leave my momma out of this and just focus on your problems for now."

Gangly shoved his way ahead, but before he could close the distance, there was a boom from overhead and a group of twelve-gauge rubber pellets slapped the man just below the neck and in the face, knocking him back and unconscious. Squatty used the distraction to try to get at Luke. He underestimated the distance and Luke easily stepped to the side, swinging the baton full force and catching the short fat man in the temple. There was a loud crack, and the fat man fell backward, his head smacking the concrete before his feet hit the ground.

Luke pivoted, holding the baton like a sword, checking his back. The girl was cowering with her hands held over her head. He looked up as a young Marine was racking a Remington 870 on the catwalk above.

"What the hell you doing down there?" the Marine said.

Luke shook his head and walked to the jug on the ground without answering. He moved to the tap and filled it before returning to the girl and handing it to her. She looked up at him with wet, tear-filled blue eyes. Up close, she looked older than she had before, or maybe the stress of the last couple weeks had aged her. Her eyes showed maturity that her face hadn't. He shook his head and looked away.

"You shouldn't have done that. I don't need trouble here," she said.

He swallowed hard and looked back at the men on the ground. They weren't moving. He relaxed his defensive posture when more Marine guards entered the tiny space. He collapsed the baton and tucked it back into the belt holster. He turned to the girl. "Don't worry about them, they won't bother you or anyone else—not anymore."

She shook her head. "The Colonel will send 'em out. They'll die. I didn't want that. These men had friends, who do you think they will blame for this?"

Luke smiled at the girl and reached out to move hair stuck to her forehead.

"What's your name?"

Her lip quivered. She looked left and right then said, as if giving up her only possession, "Kate."

"Kate short for Katherine?" Luke asked.

"Kate short for Kate," she snapped sharply.

He smiled and stepped closer, looking her in the eye. "Do me a favor, Kate, and keep worrying about people, but let me handle this. Okay? This camp is better off with those men being exiled."

The girl blinked away tears and hugged the jug of water, looking back to the men who were now on their feet, still dazed, their hands flex-cuffed behind their backs. She looked at Luke and nodded her head.

A Marine corporal approached as Luke stood, watching the men being carried off. "We'll need you to come up front and file a report on this."

Luke nodded and looked at the blue tarps. "Can you get your people to rip this shit down before they leave?"

The man stared at the tarps and nodded. "Can do," the Marine said, turning away.

"What about the girl?" Luke asked. "Any idea what her situation is?"

The Marine shrugged. "Forget about it. She isn't our problem. Let her people take care of her."

Luke frowned and stepped off toward the exit. At the end of the factory floor, the young girl stood in the walkway, blocking his path. Obviously waiting for him, she still held the water jug against her chest. He stopped and the girl moved toward him, saying, "You can't leave me here after what you did. They'll kill me."

"What I did?" Luke snapped back. "I saved you."

"I could have handled myself. I didn't ask you for help." She pointed behind him. Several men stood, leaning against a brick wall, staring back at them. "You think beating up a few punks changed anything? All you did was put a target on my head. I'm as good as dead if I go back in there."

Luke turned and stared at the men. They stared back, unintimidated. He took a step toward them and felt the girl's grip on his arm. "You going to fight them all? They run this place, they'll kill you too."

"The *Marines* run this place," Luke said, pulling his arm away. "Not a bunch of half-assed water pirates."

"No," she said, shaking her head. "Maybe at first, but not anymore. The Marines don't care as long as we stay in our own mess and don't interfere with the cops or them. They don't care what happens in here. They knew about the water, and they did nothing. They know about a lot of stuff that they don't stop."

Luke rubbed his tired eyes. He turned away from the men and looked back toward the exit door at the end of the factory. "Well, you can't come with me."

"If you leave me in here, they'll kill me. I'm all alone. I don't know anyone and everything I own is in this pack."

He shook his head, frustrated, then sighed and

looked back toward the doors. "Listen, I'll see if I can get you transferred to a different facility. But that's it; there isn't anything else I can do."

"The other building won't be any different."

"Take it or leave it," Luke said. "It makes no difference to me."

She nodded her head. "Fine then, just get me out of here."

CHAPTER THREE

North of Hayslette, Virginia

G yles knew Weaver wasn't happy about being left out of the short search patrol. There wasn't much mistaking it when his long-time friend all but refused to let him go alone. Weaver was a professional, and apocalypse or not, the man would follow orders. Gyles would have liked nothing more than to have him along, but he also needed someone to ensure the team and supplies returned to Alamo safely.

Even though Weaver was adamant about not being the one to lead that convoy, Gyles also knew his number two in command wasn't the type to disobey an order. Reluctantly, Weaver did as he was told and led the rest of the men back to camp—on one condition, and that was with standing instructions that if Gyles wasn't back by the next evening, Weaver could go out after him.

The radio squawked. "You got twenty-four hours, boss, and I'm coming to get you."

Gyles grinned and went to respond, but the speaker turned to straight static and clicks. The sign of the constant jamming. The radios were still shit. They'd made their last positive radio check, and as the range stretched, they would be on their own. The radios still wouldn't work outside of a few hundred meters.

There were plenty of rumors in the air about it; some said it was due to a nuclear reactor melting down somewhere out West and spilling radiation into the atmosphere. Others said it was because all the radio stations in the country suddenly went hot mic'd after the fall. Each idea was more insane than the next. But Gyles and several others suspected the truth—somewhere someone was jamming them because they wanted people to lock up tight and die, vulnerable and alone. Why that was, he didn't know.

He pushed back in the seat and dropped a pair of dark glasses over his eyes. In the shotgun seat of the Humvee, he propped up his rifle between his knees and focused on distant structures as they rode down the narrow city streets. The sun was shining bright, garbage littered the road, and the houses looked like any other in every small town across the USA. Nobody in sight, not a dog, not a curtain moving behind a closed window. Street after street, it was like they were on the darkest side of the moon, with no life to be seen.

There was something about the sunlight and the

heat of the day that kept the Primals hidden. The things had become nocturnal, only hunting when they were in direct contact. The things knew to stay inside and out of sight; if they popped out, they would be easy targets for the soldiers' rifles. If one was spotted, it would attack, but for the most part, they went dormant during the day. But at night was a different story... at night the things were vicious and just as rabid as they were during the first days of the infection.

He turned his head, searching the troop compartment and scanning his troops' faces. Mega, his loyal machine gunner, was over his left shoulder in the turret, rock steady with the M240. Gyles wouldn't want anyone else covering them from above. Culver, cool and collected as always, was in the back right seat, intently watching the side streets. One of the new recruits, Kenny Johansen, drove. Alvarez insisted that if they went, they take Johansen with them. He was some sort of self-proclaimed expert on the local neighborhoods. Looking at him, he didn't seem like much, but Gyles wasn't one to knock Alverez in his evaluation of soldiers.

Kenny was the boot to Reaper Platoon, but he wasn't a rookie. The man had done his time in uniform. He'd been out of the Army nearly eight years, and those years seemed to have ridden the man a bit rough. With the shortage of fighting men, the Colonel was taking anyone with military experience out of the survivors' block. With the conditions in the camp, it didn't take much coercing to get Kenny back into uniform... or at least some part of one; some bits of the uniform were harder to come by than others. He wore denim workpants with his uniform top and full body armor with all the plates scrapped out. His kit, for the most part, was in a Marine camo pattern. He'd slapped a strip of duct tape over the Marine name tape and drawn a series of smiley faces in its place.

Even dressed out and looking like a Hollywood version of a military contractor, the man still didn't think of himself as a soldier. He continued to tell the other troops of Reaper Platoon that he was just a scout. Sure, he would come along and help them out in case they got into trouble, but if something better came up, he couldn't make any promises. He laughed, comparing himself to the Kit Carson scouts that guided the horse soldiers in the Old West.

Gyles really didn't care what the man thought of himself if he followed orders and pointed his rifle in the right places at the right times. What title he used— scout, contractor, or vagabond—didn't matter much, and three weeks into the apocalypse, Gyles wasn't too concerned with blue jeans instead of camouflage trousers either. Gyles pushed back into his seat again and, without looking at his driver, said, "So tell me, Kenny, what makes you so highly recommended on this road trip? You a super-secret black ops ninja from way back when?"

The man laughed as he fished into a vest pocket and slapped on a pair of scratched aviator glasses.

"Uber," Kenny answered in a Texas drawl so thick, it almost seemed put on.

"Uber what?" Gyles asked.

Kenny shrugged and slowed the Hummer as he navigated a turn. "Uber. You know, like the car lift service—taxis. This was my area. I know the neighborhoods, I know the people. I know where all the party girls live in this town."

"You're from here then?"

"Nah." The man shook his head. "From Odessa, Texas, originally. I'm only out here because I was stationed up at Fort Lee for a minute with the Army. I met a girl that was from Middleburg after my last tour in the Sandbox. Ended up settling down with her when I left the Army."

"Middleburg, that town northwest of here?" Gyles said, remembering the name from the tactical maps in one of his many briefings.

"Yup." He shrugged. "Might as well be a thousand miles now, though, with the roads blocked the way they are. And then you never know when you'll hit one of the bands of infected."

Gyles looked out the window as the driver slowed and maneuvered along the shoulder to pass another patch of disabled vehicles. He knew what the man was saying. The infected had started to bunch up, moving in thick lines that, so far, had appeared random. It was impossible to predict when you might run into one, or when one might find you. Even in the bright sunlight, you could make a wrong turn and hit a tight pack of them just standing there.

A chance encounter during the day could be just as dangerous as at night. The Colonel's intel team did the best they could to track them, but there were still only so many eyes in the sky. Currently, a thick band was glued to the camp to their south, and from drone reports, there were more large groups scattered around the area.

He looked back at the driver. "It's not that far—Middleburg, I mean. If you think she is still there, we could try for it sometime. I could set it up. The area needs scouting, anyhow."

The man shook his head and laughed. "Nope, she ain't there no more. She was into more soldiers than just me. She liked to party and didn't care for me once I started school and had to get a job just to get by. She lost interest in me shortly after I left the Army. I was out hustling to pay the bills. Seems I was more exciting as a deployed Joe, sending money home. When I became just another run-of-the-mill civilian with a shit job, life got boring for her."

"I'm sorry," Gyles said shrugging.

"Nothing to be sorry about; she was a grade-A whore. I lucked out having her run off when she did. Sure, she left me with a load of debt and a mortgage I still can't afford, but it still beats the alternative."

"What the hell could be worse than that?" Gyles asked.

"Shit, seriously? Hell, we might have had kids

together." The man shook his head and wiped at his forehead. "Could you imagine being a father in the middle of all of this?" The man stopped and caught himself. "Hey, my bad, Sergeant. I mean, I don't even know... you don't have kids, do you?"

"It's okay, Kenny. Seems we are a bunch of bachelors in the truck today. I mean, I got a wife out there someplace. Well, had. She kind of took off and left me when I was deployed. Came home to an empty apartment and Dear John letter." Gyles shook his head and shifted the focus of the conversation back to Kenny. "So, your ex... do you know where she is at then?"

The man shrugged. "Last I heard, she was living up near Fort Meade, shacked up with some staff sergeant. No hard feelings, though. I wish her the all best—S.T.D.s, crabs, herpes, gonorrhea, all of 'em," he said, causing Gyles to laugh and breaking the tension.

Culver leaned forward between the seats. "So, wait a damn minute. You're telling me you're from Texas, but you're living in Virginia because you met a girl that now lives in Maryland with some Jody?" Culver laughed. "Now isn't that some of the stupidest shit."

Kenny laughed with them. "It is what it is, bro. I left the Army and busted my ass working my way through school. Got some silly literature degree that couldn't pay the bills, so I started driving folks around. The money wasn't bad, but it kept me busy at night, and nighttime is when Cindy liked to run and hunt for cock."

"But Maryland," Culver said. "How'd your lady get way up there?"

"I told you. She met the guy when he worked up in DC. Some intel geek, I think. When it came time for him to rotate, she went with him." He shook his head. "Seriously, fellas, it was a couple years ago. I am not one bit concerned about her."

"Was she hot at least?" Mega yelled down from the turret.

Gyles laughed and leaned back, shaking his head. "You don't have to answer that, Kenny. Mega is an animal. He wouldn't know hot if it set him on fire."

"Nah, she wasn't hot at all," Kenny laughed. "Kind of gross, even. But she did stuff, crazy stuff, so it sorta evened out."

Gyles could hear Mega's booming laugh echoing from outside the vehicle's armor. He put a hand up. "Okay, boys, we all had a good laugh at Kenny's expense. Let's get back on the job." He rolled his shoulders and investigated a dark alley as they slowly passed. "Kenny, you know where this church is?"

The Humvee slowed and rounded a corner, now moving west. Kenny nudged it along the shoulder of the road and stopped. He let the vehicle idle as he pointed a finger ahead and to the left of them. "At the intersection, we'll turn left, and you'll see a church on the right. If it's in this town then that's got to be it."

"You know the place?" Gyles asked.

"Not really. I drove past it a lot, but never had a reason to stop other than dropping off a regular grandma on Sunday morning. Mrs. Nelson. A good old gal... always weak on the tips though." He paused to think, his eyes focused on the road ahead. "You know what—the place is gated. High walls all the way around. It would be a good spot to hole up. I wasn't so sure before, if this would be the spot the note was talking about... but, yeah, thinking on it, I guess I wouldn't be surprised to find survivors in there."

Gyles nodded then brought up a pair of small scout binoculars and checked the roadway through the optics. The path ahead was narrow and cars were parked on the sides of the street, tall trees blanketing them in shade. The intersection was open. It appeared as if someone had recently cleared it by force. More cars were moved onto the sidewalks as if they'd been pushed there.

"Okay, take us up slow," Gyles said just above a whisper, his body growing tense and his free hand gripping the rifle.

The Humvee clunked back into gear and rolled forward slowly. As they neared the intersection, Gyles could see around the corner and to a tall, granite wall that ran parallel to a sidewalk. Set behind the wall was the church structure, tall and built of heavy stone that complemented the wall. Kenny let the vehicle continue its slow roll and turned north at the intersection, putting the wall just outside Gyles's window to the right.

Suddenly, Mega dropped into the vehicle and the

hatch clunked closed behind him. "Shut it down!" he said in a hoarse whisper. "Kill the engine."

Kenny hit the brake. The vehicle stopped hard.

"Shut it down; kill the engine now!" Mega repeated the order.

Gyles pointed at his driver. "Do it. Turn it off, Kenny."

As soon as the engine was silenced, Gyles heard the low moan of the infected. It was dull and far away, but he could tell from the echoes there were a lot of them. They were heavily massed somewhere close by.

"Did you see them?" Gyles asked, not looking back.

Mega crouched into the vehicle, unbuckling his gunner's harness and crammed forward between the seats. His eyes were wide and bloodshot, his head slowly shaking side to side. "I saw something, and I heard it. They are up there."

"What did you see?" Kenny asked.

Mega shot a hand and pointed directly ahead. "Out there. Look! In the shadows of the trees," the man bellowed.

Just as Gyles looked to the front, he saw a blur of movement—two figures running across the intersection. "Where are they going?" He knew if the things were moving in the daylight, there were survivors close by.

"That's the direction of the church's street gate," Kenny whispered. "You want me to keep going?"

"No," Gyles said, his head turned to focus on the wall. "If they don't see us, let's keep it that way. Can you get us closer to the wall without hitting it? I want to go over and have a look inside then meet you all back here."

"Hell no, Sergeant, not alone," Mega said. "I'll go with you."

Gyles shook his head. "I'm not going with your big, non-whispering ass. I'll take Culver, if you insist. You stay here with the vehicle, be ready to roll in a hurry if things get nutty." Gyles reached into a shelf below the military radio mounted between the front seats and retrieved a pair of civilian Motorola radios. He passed one to Kenny then clipped the other to his shirt collar. He looked back at Culver, who was checking the magazine carrier on his chest. "You ready?"

"Do I have a choice?" said the soldier from Illinois.

Gyles smiled. "You always have a choice, you just might not like the consequences of making a bad one."

Culver grinned back and dipped his chin. "In that case, let's do this."

Looking back to the driver, Gyles instructed Kenny to get them onto the sidewalk and as close to the wall as he could without hitting it. When there, Culver opened the gunner's hatch and climbed out onto the roof of the Humvee. Gyles moved out just behind him. Now next to the wall, they found the top edge just above their heads. The sounds of the infected were louder out of the protection of the armored vehicle. The sergeant slung his rifle over his back and reached out, grabbing the top of the wall with his gloved hands.

"Careful, Sarge. I heard sometimes folks embed broken glass into the tops of walls like this."

Gyles snatched his hands back and looked at his gloves then shook his head as he reached back for the wall. "We aren't in Iraq, Culver... or even worse, Chicago." He laughed. "I doubt these good Christian folks have the wall booby trapped."

Culver shrugged. "Just saying."

"Well, say less and give me a boost."

Culver did as instructed and linked his hands together; Gyles stepped into his grip and was lifted to the top of the wall. Gyles swung an arm over, once again thinking about the glass comment as he straddled the wall like a horse. He held his breath and looked down to the other side. Surprisingly, the level of the ground was higher on the far side; it was less than a four-foot drop. He dug his boots into the wall and pulled Culver up beside him. Then without wanting to stay exposed, they both dropped to the inside of the wall. Culver turned out, unslinging his rifle and aiming it toward the back of the church as Gyles did the same, looking to the front.

They sat silently listening, only hearing the moaning infected to their front. Gyles moved out a bit from the wall and knelt low in grass that hadn't been cut for weeks. They were on a long, narrow strip of lawn that ran between the church and the wall. The sanctuary was to their right, and the only windows he could see were stained glass mounted high on the structure. A cobblestone sidewalk ran along the building toward what Gyles assumed would be the main gate. He turned back and could see that the sidewalk continued and looped around the back of the church.

He reached out, tapped Culver on the shoulder, and whispered, "Lead us out. I want to get inside and see if we can find a back door."

Culver didn't look back. Keeping his eyes on his sector, he rose silently and stepped off in a crouch, patrolling forward. He moved over the sidewalk and edged close to the church structure. Gyles let him gain separation then stepped off to follow, pausing only to occasionally look behind him. He shadowed the man along the wall until they reached the corner, then held up.

Gyles closed in on Culver and stopped to listen again as he rotated and checked their back trail to ensure they were still alone. He sensed movement and flinched out away from the wall. Above them, mounted to the wall, was a single camera. He reached out and grabbed Culver's arm. The man looked back, and Gyles pointed at the camera over their heads.

"You think it's on?" Culver whispered.

"I could have sworn I saw it move."

Culver's brow tightened and he squinted as he looked at the camera, which was currently angled down at them. "You sure?"

Gyles shook his head and pointed to the camera, waving at it. He flashed a thumbs up and a smile before waving again, getting no response. "I don't know, I thought it moved." Gyles stared at the camera for a moment longer before nodding to Culver. "Screw it, let's go."

The point man stepped off again then moved out from the wall as he rounded the corner, his rifle barrel slicing the viewable area. As the young soldier moved, Gyles quickly positioned himself to cover his exposed side until they were both safely tucked back in against the next wall. With new terrain to their front, Culver only moved far enough to conceal them in a shadow then took a knee as Gyles pressed up behind him, facing their back trail. The sounds of the moaning still reached them, but it was noticeably quieter inside the walls and on the far side of the church.

Gyles surveyed the area in the back of the church. There were several covered openings, small porches that led up to heavy wooden doors. Windows placed high in the walls were covered with stained glass and decorative wrought iron guards. Farther to the back of the church grounds and out of the normal view of guests, the ornate designs were gone. The grass and cobblestone were replaced with fresh black asphalt that seemed to cover every space between the back of the church and the wall that still surrounded them. Far to the end, in the opposite corner, was a long carriage house built of stone that matched the church.

Three separate garage doors were evenly spaced in the building. Next to that was a large green dumpster and another utility shed covered in vinyl siding. Gyles watched as Culver raised his rifle and steadied it on the distant dumpster.

"That what I think it is?" Culver whispered.

"I don't see what you are looking at."

Culver pointed a gloved finger. "Between the dumpster and that garage. You see it now?"

Gyles lifted his own rifle and looked out through the scope. He scanned left and spotted it: a curled and twisted hand connected to a grey arm. Panning right, he spotted more of the twisted shapes behind the dumpster. He exhaled loudly and nodded his head. "I see it. A body drop."

"You want to go check it out?"

Gyles cleared his throat and looked back to the building and the closest entrance door. "No, we're here for the living, not the dead. As far as I know, Primals don't stack up bodies. Let's see if we can find a way inside and see who does."

Culver stood again, and this time, they moved together in a tight crouch; Culver with his rifle ahead, trained on the door, with Gyles off his right shoulder, covering the outside and sweeping to check behind them. Soon they were climbing a narrow set of steps up to a back door made of wood planks and painted a bright white. Culver moved to the right of it as Gyles positioned himself to the left. There was a sign on the door, something about clothing drop-offs and a food bank.

The young soldier reached below the sign and put his hand on the knob. He paused and made eye contact with Gyles, who nodded. He twisted the knob, but the door didn't open. Culver shook his head no. Culver reached for a tactical tomahawk on his belt, prepared to break the door in, when Gyles held up a hand to stop him.

"If there are people in there, I don't want to go busting in their door," he whispered. "Might piss them off."

"So, what then?" Culver looked at him. "You want to check for another way in?"

Gyles shook his head. "Nah," he said and rapped his knuckles on the solid surface of the planks. "Let's try this first." He knocked again and the pair listened intently. Within minutes, they heard movement inside and then the knob moved. Instead of opening, a second door farther down the wall opened and a pair of men poured out, holding shotguns and rifles to their shoulders.

"Whoa." Gyles stepped back and held up his hands, letting his own rifle hang on its sling. "We didn't come looking for trouble, gentleman."

With their attention now down the wall, the door to their immediate front opened. An elderly black man in a dark coat stepped out, holding a pistol. "And who might you be?" the man asked.

CHAPTER FOUR

DAY OF INFECTION, PLUS EIGHTEEN

Camp Alamo, Near Hayslette, Virginia

"No—absolutely not. You cannot stay here," Luke insisted.

The girl didn't budge, holding her place on a kitchen chair just inside the tiny room. Narrow and no larger than a converted storage closet, it was hardly big enough to hold a pair of duffel bags and his bedroll. Luke owned a single piece of furniture, and the girl was presently occupying it. The tiny room, located on the third floor of the camp's garrison building, wasn't much of a barracks space.

The small size of the space in this instance was a blessing to Luke, as it meant he wasn't required to have a roommate, and he really wanted to keep it that way. They'd only stopped here on the way to the admin office so he could give her some extra survival gear and a field jacket. His intent was to keep her moving so he could turn her over to the Marines. Unfortunately, that plan had stalled out, and she was now refusing to leave his room. Luke stood in the open doorway, his hand rubbing his forehead. Marines passed by, grinning at him as they glanced inside, one pumping his index finger into a balled fist.

"Fuck off, perv, she's a kid," Luke said.

The Marine laughed. "Hey, no judgment, old man."

"Old man?" Luke grimaced. "Get lost before I show you who's an old man."

The girl stomped her feet and pushed the chair against the wall. "See? Right there, even with you guys. You know what will happen to me down there in the survivors' block? You know what they'll do once they find out I'm all alone?"

"Come on, work with me here," Luke said. "I could get kicked out of this block just for having you in my room. Civilians aren't allowed up here. You think these dickheads will keep this a secret?"

"Then why am I here—*Luke?*" She said his name with contempt, shaking her head as she dropped the syllable. "I should have just stayed out there. I was better off with the monsters."

"Are you kidding me right now?" He grunted. "Fine. You stay here. I'll go live in the survivors' block. Anything has to be better than this." He moved out of the doorframe and shut it behind him. He took a few steps from the door and caught a glance from a Marine on roving guard duty. The man smirked, and Luke raised a pointed finger, cautioning him.

The young Marine grinned and showed his empty palms as a truce sign.

"Listen," Luke said, "can you keep an eye on that door? Don't let her leave until I get back."

"Whoa, whoa, whoa, I'm no babysitter," the young man said. "And I ain't down with you kidnapping no girl, either."

Luke sighed anxiously. "She's a witness in a crime."

"Then you should take her to the Colonel; you know civvies aren't allowed up here."

Luke pressed his eyes closed and tried to rub off a piercing headache. "I just need you to keep her in that room until I get back. Nail the damn door shut, if you must. I just don't want her running off or anyone messing with her. She might be in trouble."

The Marine's eyes turned to the door then looked back to Luke with concern. "Is she dangerous?"

"No, she's a damn kid."

The Marine scowled and looked at his watch. "My shift ends in an hour; that's all you got. I ain't putting this crap in the watch log, and I'm not turning it over to the next shift."

"Good enough," Luke said, moving away. He traveled along a passageway and back toward the large factory floor filled with glassed-in offices. He walked to the stairway that led up to the mezzanine offices, where he knew the command staff resided. At the end of the large bay, he saw soldiers entering from the garage bay that was now the motor pool.

He recognized several of them from Gyles's Reaper Platoon. He considered stopping by and talking out his problem with the sergeant before taking it to the camp admin, but decided otherwise. Gyles had his own real-world problems, and he'd gotten himself into this mess —he'd get himself out of it. Trying to get the girl a room would be the quickest fix.

At the end of the walkway was a double cube made of raw lumber in the middle of the factory. Before all this, it would have been an office where engineers and managers would man desk space and observe the factory floor. Now it was paneled in on all sides, the door reinforced with plywood, a large plank deck and railing surrounding it.

"Damn Seabees," he muttered to himself. The block-and-plywood construction were the telltale building style of the Navy Combat Construction men —they would wrap everything in plywood, if they could. And since the moment the camp had gone up, the Bees had been going on runs, raiding every Home Depot and lumberyard within a hundred miles before returning to make the camp look like a plywood fortress.

Luke wouldn't complain about it, though. The barricades and ramparts were impressive and, to date, not a single infected person had breached them. He moved to the door and pushed it open. As he stepped inside, a large coiled spring nearly snapped the door from his hand and slammed it shut. The inside was no more appealing than outside, a deep square of wood that smelled like a lumberyard. Behind a tall plywood counter that hadn't been there the last time he visited, were desks and tables constructed of even more plywood.

A Marine sergeant looked up at him from a back corner. Her name was Janette Acosta. She had been on duty the night he arrived and they assigned him his room. Since then, they'd somewhat become friends... if you could call being constantly harassed and mocked "friendship". She was small and wiry but had a Puerto Rican attitude twice her size. Somehow, she'd gotten it into her head that she and Luke were an item, or she was just doing it to mess with him.

Acosta moved to the counter and leaned against it. He looked away, trying to divert his eyes and not check her out. Attracted to her or not, he was still a male, and as a female, she was hitting high on the averages. "Hey, look at this. It's Deputy Luke Ross," she said in a rant heavily laced with sarcasm. "So, please tell me you finally decided to take Master Guns up on his offer to sign back in with the Corps."

Luke scowled and shook his head. "I've got a problem. I think you can help me with it."

"Oh, I'm sure I could find an officer to swear you in."

Luke grimaced. "That's not the problem."

"Problem then, huh?" She tipped her head to the

left like she was thinking. "Is it girlfriend problems because, you know, I am not playing right?"

Luke shook his head and sighed. "I picked up a girl in the survivors' block."

"Wait, so you're cheating on me then? Is that it, Luke?"

"It's not like that," Luke grunted in frustration, not amused by the game. "This kid, she was in trouble. I had to arrest a few guys messing with her, and now she thinks she isn't safe in the block."

"I heard about that, Mr. Hero. Sounded like you did a lot more than arrest them fools. I heard you nearly killed one of them. No worries about it, though. They'll be exiled by sundown. It's nothing for you to lose sleep over."

Luke shrugged. "And that's really not going to help her case with the locals. Like I said, she isn't safe in the block anymore. She fears retaliation, so I took her back to my room."

"Damn, Luke—you sure it isn't like *that*?" she said, staring him down. "You brought a girl back to your room? You gone completely loco?"

Luke looked away. When he looked back up, he could see he'd gained the rest of the admin office's attention. A young Marine private was looking at him, holding a fist and pumping an index finger. "Holy hell, what is it with you damn Marines?" Luke said. "I told you it's not like that. She was being harassed by some guys. I had to break up a fight and pull her out of there.

Now she can't return without the rest of the crew coming after her."

"Broken record," Acosta said and raised her hands, showing her palms. Luke clenched his fists and went to speak again, when she held up her palm to his face. "Calm down, hero. So, she can't go back to Block A. I can find her something in B." She grinned. "But if you can hold on to her a couple days, I might have something better."

"No," Luke snapped back quickly. "I cannot hold on to her. She needs something now, and she is refusing to go back to the survivors' blocks. Any block, for that matter."

Acosta shrugged. "Nobody is forced to stick around; send her packing. Show her the door."

"She's an unaccompanied minor, Janette." Luke knew he was taking a risk, dropping Acosta's first name in front of her Marines. Even though she played loose with formalities, she took her rank seriously.

Acosta appeared unfazed by the name drop, but Luke knew he would be catching shit for it later. The woman sighed and asked, "How old is the girl?"

He shrugged. "I don't know sixteen, eighteen maybe?"

"Which is it?" she said, her tone softening. "Big difference between sixteen and eighteen."

Luke knew he had her on the hook now. From the look on the woman's face, he could see that her gears were turning, her sensitive side waking up. Now he just had to reel her in. "I'm not sure how old, but she's a young girl all alone. You can relate, right?"

Acosta looked up at him, her brows suddenly tightened, the concerned look gone. "No, I can't *relate*. Ain't nobody messing with me."

Damn. Stupid move. Acosta can't relate to anyone, he thought to himself as the line broke and the hook was thrown into the murky depths. "Come on, just assign her a room up on the garrison deck," he said, pointing to the whiteboard with the room assignments written on it. There were still several squares showing empty or listed as supply closets. "I'll get her a job on this side. She can work in here or in the military chow hall. Help me out; I can't just ditch her."

The woman shook her head no, then turned back to face him. "Look, best I can do is find a family to try and foster her. There are plenty of kids like that in the blocks right now. Besides, no way the Colonel would allow a civilian to stay in the troop barracks."

"I'm sorry, that won't work," Luke said, turning his back to the counter.

"Luke, hold up," Acosta said. She reached down and grabbed a rifle from a rack as she rounded the wooden counter. "Let's grab a cup of coffee."

Luke tucked in his lip and nodded. "Okay."

He stepped aside and let the Marine move past him out of the wooden cube and onto the deck. He followed her out and down the steps. She waited for him in the passageway then turned to walk toward the Marine galley at the far end of the factory floor.

"I didn't know there was any coffee left in camp," Luke said.

She laughed. "There isn't, but I told my Marines I quit smoking." She kept moving and turned toward a steel shuttered door. She pulled away several blocking bars then unlocked and pulled the door open, revealing a caged-in area with several crudely constructed picnic tables. They were outside the structure, against an edge of the steel-clad building surrounded by blacktop, and in the distance, the earthen wall. Roars of the infected and diesel engines outside drifted toward them from the far side of the berm. Luke could see tall towers of heavy black smoke roiling into the distant sky.

"Even at the end of the world, the Colonel won't let us have a cigarette indoors." She waved her hand, signaling for Luke to exit.

Luke moved through the doorway and into the small chain link cube reminiscent of a prison exercise yard. He hadn't been outside since arriving to the camp; the sounds of the screams and stench of death reminded him why. The smell of the fire was stronger out here than it had been inside. The stink of diesel and burning garbage brought back memories of Iraq, where the high humidity made the stink stick and linger around his face.

Shaking his head, he turned away. Luke moved to the back and saw an empty paint can filled with cigarette butts. He stepped to a table and sat on the top of it. Acosta walked to his front and dug a pack of cigarettes from a cargo pocket on her thigh. She offered him one, but Luke declined. The woman pointed toward the roars along the south fence. "The infected are stacking up against the barriers, doubling every few hours. The numbers have gotten so thick that it's almost pointless to shoot them anymore. The Seabees are trying to move them with the dozers, pushing them into the burn pits... until they overflow."

"Does it work?" Luke asked.

She shook her head. "It was, but it sounds like the things are learning. A lot of them stay back now, moving away from the dozers. Or they get in close to the walls, where the dozers can't reach them, then rush the backs of them. They've even started to bunch up around the gates. They wait until the doors open for the dozers to leave then force their way inside. Some get in before the gates can be closed. The guards have been able to control it so far."

"They wait by the gate?" Luke asked.

She took a long draw on the cigarette and nodded. "It's like they know our perimeter, like they are learning it, and learning how we respond. We were starting fires way out in the fields to draw them off earlier." She shook her head. "It's the only thing that still seems to work, but we are running out of things to burn."

"Is this something I should be worried about?"

She shrugged, took a deep drag, then spoke. "Listen, there is something else, and I didn't want to say anything in there because I'm not really supposed to know this. Last thing we need is a panic."

Luke's brows lifted, his attention piqued. "Know what?"

She pulled the cigarette away and took a seat next to him. "They've contacted the surviving units from Fort Stewart. Some infantry guys and mechanized units with tanks and all that, like a real functioning division."

"Erickson?" Luke said, turning to face her.

"Yeah, that name sounds right. I think that was the guy." Acosta looked down at her boots. "Military forces are rallying. They've got a bunch of Rangers there, some more from the Third Infantry Division, and other straggler units coming back from the Meat Grinder. What's left of them have set up in Savanah, Georgia."

"What's left of them?" Luke said, his eyebrows turning up.

She shook her head. "It's not looking good for the home team. The Army has lost a lot of people, same as the Corps. We haven't heard anything from the Airforce and Navy."

"So what does that mean for us?"

"Nothing right now. Fort Stewart is nearly six hundred miles away. Colonel is still plotting a way for us to combine efforts. A way to get us all there. Ericson is talking about sending a bus convoy to get us all out."

"Wait," —Luke shook his head— "get us out? How is that? How did they contact Ericson? Long-range radios are down."

Acosta locked eyes with him. "Luke, you can't go spouting this stuff off. You can't tell anyone."

He nodded. "Shit, who am I going to tell?"

She grinned at him. "I've got a friend in the communications shack. There seems to be some leadership folks left alive out West trying to coordinate a counter offensive. Some military guys working out of a bunker in Colorado, not so much as helping us directly. They are mostly concerned with their own survival, but they've been helping us out with intel and tech, troop locations, stuff like that."

"But the radios—they do, or they don't work?"

"They work. Just not all the time. There is a window apparently when they open. It's random and changes every hour, but these bunker guys contacted us and passed the schedule on to Colonel McDuffie. They've been talking for almost three days now. They linked us up with Erickson."

Luke raised his hands. "Okay, this is all great, but how does any of it help me with my problem?"

"Luke, they are talking about evacuating everyone to Savannah. The infected outside is growing every day, and security is losing faith in being able to hold them back long term. As soon as the Colonel can get a convoy plan together, we are gone, bro, and soon— weeks, maybe days."

"They are closing the camp? All of it?"

She nodded her head. "Except for some transient space and a few patrol elements, it'll all be shut down. They want to increase efforts to supply up in the next few days and then bug everyone out together. We just can't do enough to stay open and feed all the refugees and fight off the infected. Fort Stewart is guaranteeing that they have a hardened perimeter. There was a FEMA staging area there, and they are heavy with supplies. They'll leave an outpost here, but everyone else will be going to Savannah."

"This isn't good. It means they are giving up on this entire region."

She looked at him sideways. "Well, doesn't this help you? That girl of yours will be getting shipped off to Savannah soon, anyhow. Cut your losses and move her into the blocks, or hold off. It really doesn't matter; we're getting out of this shithole, either way."

Luke nodded and scratched his chin. "Janette, this doesn't feel right to me. There are still people out there. If we leave, there will be nothing left for them, no chance at all. And who the hell are these people, and why are they jamming the radios still?"

She looked at him and shook her head. "I didn't tell you this so you could go second-guessing the Colonel. Don't go mouthing off and starting conspiracies of your own." She dropped the cigarette butt into the paint can and moved closer. "Listen, I only told you so you could prepare yourself and this girl if she is really that important. We will all be moving out soon. You need to pack your gear and be ready. When the order comes down, there won't be much time."

CHAPTER FIVE

DAY OF INFECTION, PLUS EIGHTEEN

North of Hayslette, Virginia

They were led down a dark hallway by men dressed in heavy clothing. They traveled through the back door and into an even darker passageway. Two additional armed men closed in behind them, pushing them forward. A sense of urgency in the air, the exit door was quickly locked and bolted, blocking the last bits of light in the confined space.

Not many words were exchanged between the strange men and Gyles. Every time Gyles had attempted get a word in, a stocky man with a pistol hushed him. Once inside, they just kept directing them deeper into the building.

As there was no effort taken to disarm them, Gyles complied and followed their instructions, signaling for Culver to stay close behind him. Moving farther into the building, the tile floors were scuffed and stained with streaks of thick blood. Flies buzzed in corners and swarmed over bits of flesh. The farther they traveled, the heavier the stench and decay became. Near the end of the hallway, Gyles noticed bullet holes in the plaster walls, blood trails, scraps of clothing, and bloodied bandages.

He stopped and looked at a shattered doorframe, running his gloved hand over the dark woodwork. There were large caliber holes and obvious signs of buckshot damage. When congealed blood touched his fingertips, he shook his head. "What is this?"

"Yeah, we had some trouble; same as everyone else," said a voice from behind. "But we don't have any infected inside, and we want to keep it that way."

Gyles stopped and looked back at the elderly black man who'd greeted them at the door. The man had a silver beard and wore a black wool watch cap. He carried a Ruger .357 Magnum service revolver as comfortably as if he'd been born with it. Gyles took his hand from the doorframe, planted his feet, and said, "I'm cool with this whole take-me-to-your-leader routine, but I have men outside. I'm not cool with leaving them out there, not knowing where I went."

"Then tell 'em, soldier," the man said, pointing to the radio on Gyles's collar. "What's keeping you?"

Gyles frowned and nodded. He took the radio handset from his shoulder and depressed the button. "Kenny, you awake?" he said and waited for a response.

The radio squelched. *"We're here boss; all clear as far as I can see. Those things haven't spotted us."*

"Okay, good. We're in the church. We've contacted friendlies; stay buttoned up and stay quiet."

"Roger that, boss."

The old man grimaced. "You could bring them inside, if you're worried about them."

Gyles shook his head no. "I don't want to put you at risk. Besides, it's good to have eyes on the street."

The man grinned but didn't say anything.

"The cameras—you already have eyes on the street, don't you? How long ago did you spot us?"

The old man laughed. "As soon as you turned onto our road, soldier boy. Seriously, let me send someone out for your men. We have a hidden gate on the side wall just behind them. Get the vehicle inside the walls, and we'll all feel better. Your boys are liable to attract unwanted attention out there, then we won't be able to help them."

Gyles sighed and looked at Culver, who shrugged. He nodded and put the radio back to his mouth. "Kenny, change of plans. Someone is going to come out and meet you. They'll guide you into the fence. Make sure Mega doesn't shoot them." He let go of the handset and waited for a response.

"Okay, boss, I'll be on the lookout for them. Mega seems disappointed though."

Grinning, Gyles said, "Understood. Stay with the vehicle until I come for you."

"Roger."

He clipped the radio back to his collar, watching the black man send one of his people back down the hall, the way they'd come. "So, who is running this place?" Gyles asked.

"Depends how you think about it, but Mister Sherman is running security. He's the one you want to talk to."

"Sherman? Is he in charge or not?" Gyles asked.

The old man laughed and waved them ahead. The group moved around a corner and to a pair of double wooden doors. The old man stepped in front of them and tapped on the ornate wooden surface then called for them to be opened. With the sounds of locks clunking and chains jingling, the hinges screeched, and the tall wooden doors pulled in. The man pointed up at the doors. "We don't even know how long it has been since those entryways had been closed. Those old things protested something fierce the first time we tried to force 'em shut."

Quickly, they were ushered ahead into a large sanctuary. Ahead of them, people were scattered around the room, some lying on pews, others in the back of the massive room, going through boxes. Gyles looked left and right while Culver moved in behind him nervously as the heavy doors were relocked.

The soldier looked back to the old man. "Where is this Sherman?"

The man holstered his revolver then pointed an index finger toward an alcove at the back of the space, where another door was hanging open. There was a guard with an AK-47 rifle posted near the opening.

Gyles took two steps in the direction then stopped and looked around the space again. "Wait, who are all of these people?"

"That's a better question for Sherman. He's up in the bell tower. Come on, I'll take you to him."

Gyles waved a hand. "Lead the way, boss."

The old man grinned and shook his head. "I ain't nobody's boss, friend. You can call me Zeke, if you'd like."

"All right, Zeke, lead the way then."

The man smiled and stepped off. While Culver took position behind him, Gyles noticed the other men had dispersed back into the sanctuary area. Whoever was running this place trusted them. They seemed to be conditioned to uniformed soldiers on the grounds. They'd allowed them to keep their weapons, and now they were being left unguarded with only an elderly man as an escort.

Weaving through people down the center aisle of the church, they reached the alcove. This time, Zeke stepped aside and waved Gyles in ahead of him. Gyles hesitated in the doorway, looking up, checking out the space before he entered. The stairs were made of well-polished white stone, the walls painted a heavy cream color that contrasted with a dark mahogany handrail. From above, the stairwell was filled with bright sunlight.

The young man with the AK-47 nodded as he

moved farther aside, and Gyles cautiously stepped into the stairway and began making his way up. In the confined space, he instantly picked up on the howling of the infected. The noises seemed to be focused and directed to him. Gyles froze and looked back at Culver behind him, who gripped his rifle at the tension in his leader's eyes.

Zeke, farther down the stairs, said, "Don't worry about it; the howling gets louder the closer we get to the front of the building. The bell tower tends to channel the noise down the stairwell."

"Creepy as hell, is what it is," Culver mumbled.

Laughing, Zeke said, "Yeah, I tend to agree, but there is no better place on the grounds to keep watch."

Gyles grunted and continued climbing. After several flights and the appearance of stained-glass windows in the walls, Gyles realized they were somewhere in the front right quadrant of the building. They passed another heavy door that matched the one at the bottom and entered a small cubed room. On first appearance, Gyles thought it looked like a well-planned guard tower. The room was at least twenty feet by twenty feet with unfinished plank floors and an enormous black bell hanging high over their heads. The walls were open air, void of glass windows, overlooking the expansive grounds of the church and city around them.

The tower's floor was filled with men, lawn chairs, and folding tables. When Gyles entered the room, they all briefly took notice then went back to whatever it was they were doing before he entered. Again, he had the feeling these people were accustomed to seeing soldiers. No mystery on their faces, they appeared bored in seeing him. On any other day, in any other place, it would have looked like a BBQ, based on the way the men carried on like everything was normal. A tall bean pole of a man with a jet-black goatee and greased-back hair ended his conversation with another and walked toward them. He locked his eyes, measuring Gyles up, before stretching out his hand. "You're new. What happened to Lieutenant Floyd?" he scoffed.

Gyles kept silent, not wanting to give anything away before he knew what was going on.

The man shrugged and said, "Name's Sherman. We were wondering when the Army would come back. Thought you all might have abandoned us."

"Back?" Gyles said, shaking the man's hand.

The man frowned and looked at Gyles sideways then locked on his name tape. "Yeah, that's right... ahh... Sergeant Gyles. You're with the National Guard, right? The delivery is late. People were starting to worry."

"Delivery? What exactly were you expecting?"

Sherman frowned and diverted his eyes to Zeke. "You aren't here to make the FEMA delivery?"

"Sorry, friend," Gyles said, shaking his head. "We're scouts from a place about twenty miles south. We didn't have any knowledge of units operating up here, much less a FEMA camp."

Sherman made a fist and bit at his knuckle. He turned and looked to the window before turning back to Gyles. "The National Guard has been bringing us supplies and transporting local survivors back to the camp. Not much to brag about, but food and medical supplies, and with the number of survivors we've been taking in, we need everything we can get. They pick up people and leave us enough to get by until the next run."

Zeke stepped forward. "I told you these soldiers are not part of the Guard; they seemed surprised to even find us here."

Gyles nodded and frowned. "Sorry—I'm not with them. Do you know where they went? If people are still operating up here, it could help all of us out."

Sherman shook his head and walked toward a window. "For all I know, they joined that party of psychopaths down there. Everything around here seems to be dying. I thought it would turn around by now. But the last day or two, it's been getting worse."

Gyles moved up beside the man. Looking through the tower openings, he had a commanding view of the main gate below and the hundreds of infected surrounding it. His eyes were drawn to a cluster that Sherman was pointing to. He spotted a dozen uniformed infected. Looking out over the city rooftops, he could still see signs of lingering smoke and the ruins of taller buildings in the distance. Along a wide main road, a parade of the infected was moving in their direction. "Shit, how long has it been like that?" Gyles asked.

"Couple days now. The pack is growing... slow at first, but since dawn, it's been doubling in size nearly every hour." Sherman moved away from the window and pulled up a lawn chair, signaling for Gyles to take one across from him. The man reached into a red cooler and tossed Gyles a bottle of water and then another to Culver. "The National Guard was holding a railroad crossing about a mile north, small tent city and camp. It was a good chokepoint and kept most of the demons out of this neighborhood. We hadn't really seen much activity in this area, so survivors tended to find their way here. Every couple of days, the Guard would convoy in, pick people up, and take them somewhere farther west, to a FEMA camp."

"And they just left it, the roadblock? They just abandoned it without warning?"

Sherman shrugged. "No idea. They didn't exactly check in with us before going silent. We have radios, but the damn things only work for a couple blocks. They bailed out the night before last. Raised one hell of a ruckus doing it too. There was a rolling gunfight over there as they left town. It wasn't planned, from what we could tell, just pure chaos. Then a bit after midnight, everything went quiet, lights went out. It got scary dark over there. Then sometime the next morning, these guys in uniform and their buddies started straggling in and surrounding the place. Crowd has been building ever since."

Gyles moved back to the window and looked out over the crowd of infected. The group was bunched up and milling around the main gate. Not pushing against it, just gathering there like they were waiting for it to suddenly open and start serving lunch. Looking at a wide street to the north, more were slowly headed in their direction, but none of them moved past the group at the gate. "Why do they all stop here?"

"Smart ones," said a man at the opposite end of the tower deck. He was sitting low in a folding chair. Nearly bald with mottled hair on the sides of his head, the man was as old, if not older, than Zeke. He was wearing a vintage army field jacket and holding binoculars to his eyes. Gyles caught notice of a well-worn M1A1 paratrooper rifle leaning against the old man's chair. The man lowered his binoculars and looked back at the others. "There isn't no logical reason for them to stop here."

Sherman grunted. "This here is Lawson. As you can see, he is a bit salty and opinionated."

"Then you tell me why they're bunching up out there," Lawson said. "Tell me why they all stop right here at our gate."

Culver leaned forward, looking at the street. "Well, they probably followed someone," he said then looked away like he'd wished he hadn't spoke.

The old man smiled and shook his head in disapproval, a deep scowl forming on his face. "Nope—we haven't made any noise to lead them here. We haven't been outside the gates in near two days. We keep the lights off, we keep the noise down. We gave no sign. I'm telling you, it's the smart ones. The smart ones are leading them here."

Gyles rubbed at his chin. "And what exactly is a smart one? I haven't seen them do anything more than run toward the sounds of people."

"Not anymore," Lawson said. "Can't put my finger on it, but some of them seem to still have something cooking upstairs. Not like human, but maybe like a wounded animal. Maybe the church means something to them, so they gather up here. But I don't think that's it. I'm sure one of them down there knows we're inside. I know those ones in uniform knew we were here. I recognize some from the convoy drops. Then again, maybe they're just assholes."

"Assholes, huh? That's some theory," Gyles said.

Lawson sighed. "Maybe some of them been watching this place all along, knew we been here all this time and were just waiting for those others to breach the roadblock so as they could have a go at us."

"All right, Lawson," Sherman said, raising a hand. "We been over this. Those things don't have much more sense than a rabid squirrel, and they certainly don't wait for reinforcements."

Lawson shook his head. "Underestimating your enemy is what gets men killed on the battlefield. We should be packing up and getting the hell out of here."

"Maybe so, but that isn't no battlefield down there. It's hell, and those are the demons," Sherman spat back.

"You're so full of shit, Sherman." Lawson waved a hand at him and grunted, going back to his binoculars.

Sherman turned back to Gyles. "So, you aren't here for the supply drop, and you aren't with the National Guard. Why are you here?"

Gyles reached into a shirt pocket, pulled out the folded cardboard scrap, and passed it to Sherman. "We found this at a market south of here. It was nailed to a telephone pole outside the grocery store. Did you put it there?"

Taking the worn cardboard and holding it between his fingers, Sherman rubbed his thumb against the worn text. "Father Andre hung these up back in the days after it all started." He closed his eyes and slowly opened them. "People gathered here then. We got them fed and the National Guard helped transport them to the FEMA camps." The man looked down at the note again, folded it, and placed it on a table. "That was when the roadblock first went up. Anyone looking for shelter done found one by now. So you said you were at the market?"

Gyles nodded.

"You happen to talk to Flynn and his crew? They should be able to help us with our food situation, if you can get word to them for us. Let him know we could use whatever they can spare."

The soldier shook his head. "I'm sorry, when we searched the market, the place had been overrun. Everyone inside was dead or turned. We didn't see any sign of survivors."

"Damn shame. They had some good folks in that camp," Sherman said. "How were they doing on supplies? Not to sound callous, but we could use them, and obviously it won't do them any good now."

Gyles shook his head. "We were there for the same reason, actually. Anything salvageable we loaded up and trucked back to our camp." He caught the suspicious look on the old man's face. "I'm with a unit south of here. We have a large survivors' camp. You all are welcome to come back with us. We have a well-guarded compound, and there's plenty of room."

Sherman laughed. "I'm not interested in being moved to one of your camps. I tried that for a minute, and it didn't work out." He looked hard at Gyles. "But what we could use is some of those supplies you stole from us."

"Stole?" Gyles asked. "When we rolled in, nothing was sitting on those supplies but a load of infected."

"Flynn was one of us. That market was part of my network; you had no business taking our goods," Sherman said, his voice rising.

Gyles raised his open hands and shook his head. "Okay, I've heard enough. We didn't come here to fight. We came to find survivors and give any assistance we could." The sergeant looked back at Culver, who was standing nervously by the door. "Listen, if you don't want our help, that's fine. We can roll out. I'll give you our location in case you change your minds. When I get back to camp, I'll give the commander your information."

Lawson stood. Holding the rifle in his right hand, he took a step towards Gyles, causing the young soldier to tighten the grip on his own rifle. "Dammit, Sherman, you better listen to these boys. We can't stay here, and you know it. We ain't got but a couple days' food left, and if we wait much longer, those things will have us blocked in."

"Lawson, sit down," Sherman shot back.

"The hell I will. I got family down there too—shit, all of us do—I ain't letting them starve over your stubbornness." Lawson waved his hand over the other men, who had all turned in their chairs to focus on the argument. "We have as much say in this as you do."

Gyles let go of the rifle and raised his hands in surrender. "We didn't come here to argue. We're leaving—you all can follow us back if you want. Or if it's easier, we can send a convoy back for you."

"Nobody is leaving," Sherman said.

Gyles could see that Lawson's jaw was quivering. The old man wanted to speak but, instead, he took a step back toward the open windows. He looked down into the street then turned back quickly. "You need to take them downstairs, show 'em," Lawson spit. "Show 'em why it is you are refusing to leave. Then look at this crowd out here and explain to the people in the church what you plan to do about it."

Sherman dropped his chin and took a step back. "You brought it up, you show 'em."

The old man scoffed before he turned away and walked toward the stairwell, dropping inside.

Zeke moved away from the door and placed a hand on Gyles's shoulder. "Come on, son, I think we're done here. You should be heading out before it gets dark."

"Nope," Lawson said.

The man slung his rifle across his back and grabbed a worn trucker's cap from the back of the chair he'd been sitting on. "We aren't even close to being done. Come on, boys. You all are going to want to see this, and I hope you brought a toothbrush because you won't be leaving tonight."

CHAPTER SIX

DAY OF INFECTION, PLUS EIGHTEEN

Camp Alamo, Near Hayslette, Virginia

Luke sat alone at a table in the galley. Using a fork, he pushed around bits of instant macaroni and cheese, separating it on his plate from some sort of reconstituted beans. Shaking his head, he looked up as a group of dusty soldiers crowded into the galley line.

The men were laughing and joking, mocking a soldier near the front who had apparently pissed himself over something that had happened on the road. Sergeant Weaver moved to the front of the line of Reaper Platoon, telling them to keep it down. He looked toward the galley and caught Luke's eye. Weaver grinned and offered a mock salute. Slapping a man next to him, he walked away from the line and took a spot at Luke's table.

"Don't miss chow on my account," Luke said.

"I'm not missing anything, that's for damn sure," Weaver laughed, pointing at Luke's tray of slop.

"We had a good supply run. I had some jerky and whatnot on the ride back. I probably shouldn't be having double rations, anyhow."

Luke nodded. "Good run... then where's Gyles? I was looking for him earlier."

The sergeant shook his head no. "He stayed out, following a lead." He looked at his watch. "Starting to make me a bit nervous, actually. He should have been back by now."

"Lead? What kind of lead is worth following out there?"

Weaver sighed and shook his head again. "He thinks there might be survivors holed up in some church. He wanted to go check it out."

"Thought you all were the hunter-gatherers in this camp. The Marines do the search and rescue."

"Yeah, try telling that to Gyles. The guy does what he wants, when he wants."

Luke nodded and pushed his tray away. Before he could take his hand off it, Weaver had the tray pulled in front of him. He lifted the fork and took a heaping mouthful of the macaroni and bean mixture. Weaver scowled and shook his head. "Just awful," he gagged before shoveling in another mouthful.

Putting up his hand, Luke smiled. "Be my guest." He paused then looked left and right. "Listen, Weaver, there is something else, something I might need some help with."

71

Weaver dipped his chin, chewing heavily. He gulped down a swallow. "Sure, brother. You're practically a member of the Reapers, whatever you need."

"What do you know about a plan to relocate out of here?"

Weaver's brow tightened. He placed the fork down beside the tray and reached for a bottle of water attached to his vest. "I've heard rumors of a plan to move everything south if we can't keep up with the provisions." He took a big gulp of water and wiped his face with his sleeve. "If we cannot find enough food around here to keep everyone fed, the Colonel won't have any other choice but to move them. And to be honest with you, Luke, numbers of the infected are growing every day. They could breach these walls if they hit us in force. Food, we can find plenty of, but bullets and fuel are growing scarce. I wouldn't mind getting some distance on them."

Rolling his shoulders, Luke leaned forward. "What if I told you it's not a rumor? It's about to happen any day now."

"I'd say good." Weaver shrugged. "I'm sick of this place."

"Good ... even knowing there are more survivors out there, people we could help? Hell, even I got family out there somewhere."

"Can't help people we can't find. Radios are down, and every place we search is abandoned or full of the dead."

"Radios aren't down," Luke said. "They are just being jammed."

Weaver sighed and sat back in his chair. "Yeah, I heard all the conspiracy on that too. But the radios aren't jammed, Luke; everyone is just dead. Sorry, friend, I know you got family out there, but nothing we can do."

"If they were just dead, you'd be able to talk to Gyles right now. They are being jammed." Luke scowled and slid closer. "Listen to me, the radios are working just fine. The Colonel is in open communication with Fort Stewart. Like I said, they're jamming everyone else. Why? I don't know, but it's happening."

"Bullshit ... now you listen, brother. If you are asking for us to help you search for your family, I've got to say no. Friend or not, all my people got family out there, alive or dead. I can't ask them to do that for you."

"Weaver, shut up for a second and listen." Luke shook his head. "What I'm trying to tell you is I think I know how I can shut the jamming off. Shut if off for good, and at least give people a chance."

"You're talking about people that might not even be out there."

"Like the ones Gyles went after today?" Luke clenched his fists. "Let me put it to you like this—in a few days, we're all going to be told to abandon this place and move south. I won't be going with them. If you change your mind, look me up."

"So, on your own, you're just going to leave this place behind?"

Luke closed his eyes and dipped his head down to the floor. "I'm not alone. I've picked up a dependent, somehow. She'll probably be going with me."

"Dependent?"

"Yeah, some damn kid followed me home and won't leave me alone."

Weaver shook his head. "Okay, hold up, brother, what exactly is going on?"

The lights suddenly snapped off then popped back on, buzzing as they flickered at a noticeably dimmer level. Weaver reached for the radio at his collar and turned up the volume, hearing a series of emergency codes. At the same time, Marines in the galley pushed away from the tables and ran back toward the barracks area.

Luke's eyes followed them. "And what's this?"

The men from the Reaper Platoon left the chow line and were gathering around their squad leader. "Looks like they're having a rush on the perimeter fences. They routed generator power to focus the spotlights out front to try to draw the infected toward the burn trenches."

"Will that work?" Luke asked.

Shrugging, Weaver looked up as the lights flickered again. "Depends on the numbers." He turned back to his men. "Listen, guys, I know we were supposed to be off mission tomorrow, but get rested up and be ready to go back out. If Sergeant Gyles isn't back before sunup, we're going out after him at first light." The men grunted and quickly dispersed. Weaver turned back to

Luke. "You still have access to that big ass MRAP of yours?"

"The Beast." Luke smiled. "I'm not about to let anyone take it."

"Then how about you gas it up and be ready to roll out with us? Take that kid if you have to."

Luke grimaced. "You think the Colonel will just let us roll away from camp? He has pretty strict orders about us staying inside."

A burst of machine gun fire echoed off the walls. From the sound, it was just outside the structure. "I'd say they're too busy to worry about it. Have your bags packed and be in the motor pool at dawn."

CHAPTER SEVEN

DAY OF INFECTION PLUS EIGHTEEN

North of Hayslette, Virginia

At the rear church parking lot, Gyles stood with the rest of his men around the armored Humvee. The white garage building was behind them, and the stone walls surrounded them on all sides. The roars of the infected seemed to be growing louder every minute they were there. The things had moved beyond the face of the church and were slowly surrounding it. If they wanted to leave now, they would have to fight their way out.

Something bad was going on here. The men holding the church seemed confident, but Gyles could see the desperation in the eyes of the families inside. He'd been to enough refugee camps to recognize the looks of terror. This wasn't the sanctuary it appeared to be at first glance; this was a lifeboat surrounded in a sea of death. If the National Guard had really pulled out, they were stranded here, and the situation would only get worse as more infected moved in. He closed his eyes, listening to the howls of the infected.

Zeke noticed his worried expression and gave him a knowing nod. "They grow more agitated as the sun goes down. I hope you all weren't planning on leaving here tonight."

Gyles moved close to the Humvee, unsnapped his rifle from its sling, and laid it on the hood of the vehicle. Mega was up in the turret, leaning back, rubbing the M240 machine gun with an oiled cloth. Culver and Kenny were both sleeping inside the crew compartment. "I have to say, Zeke, we were planning on leaving. I have people waiting on me back at base. So, if you don't produce this whatever it is Lawson wanted us to see, I think we'll be saying our goodbyes."

Zeke laughed and nodded his head. "I get your impatience, but it'll be worth it. And shouldn't be much longer. Father Andre isn't the man he used to be, but I'm sure once Lawson breaks things down to him, he'll be willing to speak to you. And better yet, willing to listen."

"Now hold up," Gyles said, stepping closer to the older man. "I thought Sherman was in charge. How the hell does this Andre figure into things?"

"Father Andre," Zeke said, correcting him with a stern look. "This is Father Andre's church. Sherman might be the man responsible for saving it, but do not be fooled, son. This congregation belongs to Father Andre. What he says, goes, regardless of how much bitching Sherman does. The people in there won't move a finger unless Andre gives the go-ahead. And worse yet, they won't leave unless Andre leads them out the door."

"Is that what this is about? Getting the people to leave?" Gyles put his hands on his hips and looked up at the darkening sky. He slowly shook his head side to side. "Listen, Zeke, you all sound like good people, and I want to help, but I'm not a salesman. I told you what we have to offer, and that's all I got—"

Zeke interrupted him. "This isn't about making deals, Sergeant. We have a lot of people inside there that need help. Sherman won't say it, but he knows we're in trouble here. Just give Father Andre a chance. Talk to him, help him make a wise decision."

The back door to the church opened again and Lawson stood in the opening. "Come on in and bring all of your people and gear. We won't be securing the grounds once we seal these doors again. The demons are still crowding in. We think it's best to lock ourselves inside. And you all shouldn't be on the road after dark."

Before Gyles could protest, Zeke had a hand on his shoulder. "He's right. You'll never make it once the sun goes down. What kind of host would we be to send you out in this weather, anyhow?" The old man half smiled, pointing toward the source of the howling.

Mega released the machine gun off the mount and jumped from the hatch, dragging an assault pack and sleeping bag behind him. "That works for me, friends. I'm tired of the food in the camp." He smiled and looked at Zeke. "Say, you got any of that Jesus juice in there? Is this one of those wine churches?"

"You a Catholic, son?" Zeke asked.

"I am tonight, brother." Mega's face turned serious. "I mean, if you got it. You weren't joking, were you?"

Lawson coughed and shook his head. "We ain't got none of that wine, but we got some brandy that I think will cleanse your soul."

Mega turned and slapped Gyles on the shoulder. "Damn, I think I been born again! I done found my people." He moved off toward the door, following Lawson inside.

Gyles waited for Culver and Kenny to move out before he did the same, leaving Zeke behind him to secure the space. This time when they moved down the hallway, instead of going to the end and into the main body of the church, they turned to a narrow passageway that wrapped behind the alter. Stopping in a dark room, Gyles followed close as they moved to a tight staircase and into a musty basement. Gyles ran his hand along the wall, noticing the heavy scarring and crumbling masonry, obvious damage from gunshots. The floor was stained with blood.

A heavy wood door marked with scratches was at the bottom of the stairs. To the left of the door, the passageway continued off into the darkness. Lawson turned back and, seeing the concerned expression on Gyles' face, said, "This entire section of the church was filled with demons when Sherman arrived. It took a lot of blood, but they got them all out."

"That explains the body pile out back, I guess," Gyles said, his expression staying hard.

Biting at his bottom lip, Lawson nodded. "You saw that, did ya? Well, that only explains half of it." Lawson took his hand off the door and turned back. "When Sherman got here, this place was completely overrun. Him and some others fought their way inside, killing everything as they went. Even Sherman says he thought everyone was dead until he heard the shouts coming from below. That's when he found Andre and most of the church members holed up behind this door."

"So, this is a safe room?"

The man shook his head no.

Gyles pointed into the darkness where the hallway continued. "And what's down there?"

"Nothing, it's all unfinished spaces and remnants of the old foundation. Sherman cleared it out. There's nothing there."

Gyles stared into the darkness, using a flashlight to try to see the end. Finally, he nodded and looked back at the door. "Why are the others upstairs, while the quasi leadership is down here hiding behind a door?"

Sighing, Lawson turned back and pounded on the door. "That, my friend, is a great question. I think it's better if you just meet Andre. I'd rather you develop your own opinion of him."

After a brief pause, a wooden trap slid in the top of the door, exposing a young man's eyes. He looked at Lawson and surveyed the uniformed men standing behind him. After a series of clunks, the door opened inward and the young man ushered them all inside before locking the door behind them. "Sorry for all the opening and closing and locking of doors," he said. "Mr. Sherman, our security man, was in the Navy, and he insists that this is how it's done to secure the ship."

Gyles stepped inside and surveyed the space. It was in stark contrast to the hallway they'd just left. The room was ornate, with walls made of precision-cut stone and furnished with dark, polished wood and overstuffed chairs, and carpets covering the floor. "Is this a ship?" Gyles asked.

The young man turned his head to the side in thought. "As Mr. Sherman says, we are securing compartments from flooding—only now the flooding is from demons instead of water."

"That makes sense," Gyles said, shaking his head. "And are you Father Andre?"

"Oh no, call me Jacob. I am Father Andre's assistant. Please, follow me. Your men can rest here. I will have food and water brought to them shortly."

Looking back, Gyles was prepared to argue the request but could see that his men were already dropping into the comfortable-looking chairs. He nodded to the young man and was led to another tall door made of mahogany. The man turned a key and ushered Gyles in ahead of him. He was greeted with a short bald man wrapped in a black robe. The man was sitting behind a dark desk, reading a leather-bound book. The walls of the room were covered with bookshelves and had no windows. In a corner of the room, he spotted Sherman sitting at a table, sipping from a porcelain cup.

The young man went to close the door, but Gyles reached out a hand, stopping him. "Sorry, friend. I'd like to leave the path open, if that's okay."

Jacob looked at the man in the black robe, who nodded his approval. The young man smiled and removed his hand from the door, crossing them to his front.

Gyles surveyed the space. "Nice office, Padre."

"Oh, this is not my office. This is the church archive and study. It's a reading and mediation room of sorts and just happens to be the safest spot on the church grounds."

Gyles looked left and right again, then up at the ceiling made of thick beams and planks. "Is there another entrance?"

"Oh no, that door is the only way in or out. It is very sturdy, I can assure you," Andre said. "Like I stated before, we are completely safe in here."

"If this church was overrun, this room would become a tomb," Gyles said. "I'd rather be outside."

"Yes, most likely there would be no escape for us, that is true," the man said. "But, same as last time, God willing, someone would come for us."

"The last time?" Gyles asked. "You mean when they had to fight their way in to free you? You would put others at risk to save you?"

"That is hardly a fair assessment." The priest stood

and walked around the wooden desk. He pointed to a pair of chairs with a small table separating them. On the table was a coffee pot and white porcelain cups. "Please sit," the man said. "Last time I had to seek refuge in this room, it was Mr. Sherman and his friends who came and let me out."

Gyles hesitated before removing his shooting gloves. He stuffed them into his shirt pocket and sat back on a red velvet-lined chair. The priest nodded toward Jacob, who turned and left the room, leaving the door open.

"I know it doesn't seem like it, but I really don't have a lot of patience," Gyles said.

Father Andre smiled and poured a cup of coffee, which he handed to Gyles before sitting in a chair across from him. "When this all started, I was like you. I was in a hurry. Always in a hurry to attend meetings, services, funerals, weddings. Every day something was happening here or there, something I had to attend to. The birth of a child, a parishioner in the hospital. I was always quick to act, to try and help." The man paused a beat and looked toward the open door then back to Gyles. "In the time since, I have found that swift decisions often come with regrets."

"I'm sure we all have regrets," Gyles said.

"There is no urgency in this. We have to just wait for it to be over." Andre smiled and looked down at his hands crossed in his lap. "Where were you when all of this started?"

Gyles looked over at Sherman. The man hadn't

budged, still staring down at the coffee cup in his hands. "A bit north of here."

"Please share, and what was it you were doing, *north of here?*"

Gyles exhaled. "My unit was sent to escort some medical people back to a base in Georgia."

"And did you?"

The soldier shook his head. "No, we didn't."

"Why not?" Andre asked.

Frowning, Gyles shrugged. "It didn't work out." He lifted his arm and circled. "All of this happened, I guess."

"And now you are here."

Gyles nodded. "Yeah,"—he exhaled—"now I'm here."

"See? We really are not that different; my story is the same as yours. I woke up one day, all of this happened—as you say—and look, now I am here." The priest smiled again. "The same as you. Not that different, are we?"

Gyles lifted the cup and took a long sip. Holding it in his hand, he looked at the priest. "Padre, I enjoy a good lecture as much as the next guy, but really, what is going on here? Is there something we can help you with, or did I waste my time stopping?"

Andre frowned and pursed his lips. "Mr. Sherman has informed me that the Army resupply missions have stopped, and he has no information on them starting again. He seems to think we need to leave this sanctuary. He tells me we may not have enough stores to last us until order is restored."

With raised eyebrows, Gyles looked across the table at Andre. "Order restored? What do you think is going on out there? Who is going to restore order?"

"Patience, my friend, this didn't happen overnight. It won't be restored overnight." The Priest pointed his hands toward the ceiling. "Of course, there is chaos, disorder, but nothing that cannot be sorted out. And when it is, the Church will be prepared to lend assistance. Just as before all of this, we will open our doors to those who need us."

Gyles studied the man's expression. He turned to Sherman, who was grinning slightly from one side of his mouth. "Listen, Padre, I think things are a bit worse than that. Yes, the National Guard or whoever it is you were dealing with, they are most likely gone." Gyles put up his hands. "Hell, they're probably all dead. I've been running patrols outside for close two weeks. I've seen no signs of police or government. As far as I can tell, everything outside is dead or dying."

"You shouldn't lose faith so quickly. As recently as a few days ago, we put people on busses to the FEMA camps. We are very safe here and will be for as long as necessary."

"And have you heard from them? These people you sent out, has any word come back from any of them?"

"I'm certain you are aware that phones and other forms of communication are not working."

Gyles shook his head and looked at Sherman. "Is he serious?"

Sherman bit at his lip and nodded. "Oh yeah, he's serious. Father Andre here believes everything is going back to normal any day now. We just have to wait and see."

"And that's why you didn't take me up on the offer to leave?" Gyles asked Sherman, ignoring the priest in front of him. "This guy is calling the shots. You're betting everyone's lives on an old man hiding in a cellar."

Sherman laughed. "Half the people upstairs, including my wife and daughter, aren't going anywhere without Andre here, and Andre says he isn't leaving this room."

Looking over his shoulder at Mega in the next room, Gyles turned back to Sherman. "I have a couple hundred pounds of dumb muscle in the other room that could get this man on a truck."

"You don't think I've thought of that?" Sherman said, shaking his head. "We try forcing this man out, we'll have a riot on our hands. People out there think this man is the reason they're still alive. You want them to go with you, then convince Andre to go."

Andre stood and smiled, completely unfazed by what the men were saying. His mood was almost childlike, as though he hadn't heard any of the conversation. "It's okay, there is no need to be anxious."

Gyles looked at the priest's face, studying him.

"What happened to you? Is it the shock of it all? When did the lights go out on your reality?"

Andre's head pulled back in confusion. "Nothing has happened to me."

Shaking his head, Gyles turned back to Sherman. "You said *half*. What about the people that do want to leave? If you have folks ready to go, I'm willing to take them out."

"Sure," Sherman said, nodding. "Lawson, his family, they are more than ready to go. Half the shooters in the tower will leave as soon as I give the word. But I can't just abandon the rest. I won't abandon the rest."

"But would you force Lawson and the others to stay, based on the words of this guy?"

Sherman shook his head. "Of course not, but it still isn't that easy."

"Tell me," Gyles said. "What is it you need from me?"

"We don't have transportation, and half those people are seniors. They can't walk out of here," Sherman said. "We had a couple busses, but the Guard commandeered those for their own evacuation missions, and they never brought them back."

"We could probably find some trucks; there are plenty of vehicles on the road."

"And then we would still have the infected to deal with," Sherman said, shaking his head. "I hate to admit it, and as much as I want to leave, I have to say Andre is right—we can't leave. We're stuck here."

Gyles looked at Andre, who sat with the same childlike smile on his face, sipping from his cup. "Yeah, this cat isn't right about anything." He set his own cup back on the table and stood. "I'll give you until morning to get your house in order."

Frowning, Sherman looked down. "By morning, we will be surrounded six-deep. If we're lucky, the walls will hold, and they'll still be outside. If not, they'll be at the church doors. We can seal up tight and hold them off until they leave."

"If you knew we would be trapped, then why the hell did you keep us here?" Gyles said, turning to investigate the room behind him. "We could have gone for help."

Andre spoke up at this. "You'll be fine, son. Please be patient."

Gyles shook his head in frustration. He looked at Sherman. "You got the wrong guy. I tried the shelter-in-place, hold-the-fort thing once."

"And?" Sherman asked.

"They all died," Gyles said, leaving the room.

CHAPTER EIGHT

DAY OF INFECTION, PLUS EIGHTEEN

Camp Alamo, Near Hayslette, Virginia

As Luke approached the top of the stairs, the gunfire outside the walls had increased; there was no ignoring the danger. Marines in full kit were pouring out of barracks rooms and forming up in the aisleways. Luke could feel the energy in the air... bad things were happening. He moved around the hustling Marines and headed to his door halfway down the narrow walkway. A Marine sergeant reached out and grabbed his arm. Luke snapped at the contact. The Marine flinched and pulled back his arm. "Hey, deputy, I hear you were one of us once."

"Once a Marine, always a Marine," Luke responded sarcastically. Seeing the concerned look on the sergeant's face, he softened his tone. "Yeah, I did my time. I'm out and not going back to it."

"I see," the sergeant said, turning back to where several other Marines were lining up.

This time it was Luke who reached out. "What's going on out there? I haven't heard this much gunfire in the camp before."

Shaking his head, the sergeant turned back, his face pale. "It's bad. They're moving at us, en masse. Something shifted them back from D.C. and they're all turning southwest. The Brass says the things are migrating, looking for food. They've already surrounded most of the camp and are pushing at the gates. They've crammed up against all the perimeter fences and are piling up against the wire fencing at the top of the berms. If we can't get out there to fight them, they'll breach those fences and, soon after, the crazies will be inside."

"How long have we got?"

The young Marine looked down at his boots and slowly shook his head side to side before returning his gaze to Luke. "It's like they know... they know our weak spots. Like they know that if they pressed up against the gates, we won't be able to get outside to stop them. And every time we open them, they rush at us."

"If you can't get outside, then where are all of you going? What's the plan?"

"Colonel is sending us to the south wall. He's hoping if we fight them there, make a lot of noise, it will draw the things around and clear up the gates on the north side."

"I thought that's what the dozers were doing out there, keeping them occupied and off the walls."

The Marine shook his head. "They got bogged down and had to evac the crews. There are so many out there, and the numbers are multiplying by the hour."

"This is bad," Luke said, rubbing his chin. He turned back to the Marine. "Take care of your men, Sergeant."

The man nodded and walked away, leaving Luke alone outside his door. He moved closer and could see that it was still closed. The Marine boot he'd talked to earlier was still standing beside it. "Thought I only had you until the end of your watch," Luke said, stopping beside him.

The kid shrugged. "Well, she tried to leave about twenty minutes after you left. It didn't feel right letting her out to wander off with everything that's going on. Anyhow, my unit is moving out; she's all your problem now." The man slung his rifle and walked away.

Luke reached for the knob and pushed, with the door resisting. He shoved again, but it wouldn't move. He knocked and shouted, "Come on... open up! It's me, Luke."

He pushed again, and when the door wouldn't open, he hit it with his shoulder. The door gave in with the cracking of wood. Moving inside, he could see that his only chair, which had been pressed against the knob, was now in a shattered heap. The girl was against the far wall, sitting with her pack in her lap. He looked at her then moved to a locker and opened it, pulling his own pack.

"Good, you're already packed," he said, grabbing his bed roll. He wrapped it up and strapped it to the top of his pack. He turned back to her. "Anyone you need to say goodbye to?"

"Are we going somewhere?" she asked, looking at him in surprise.

He stood and walked toward the doorway. "Oh yeah, we're going—and most likely not coming back."

"What makes you think I'm going with you?" she said, not moving from her spot.

Luke shrugged. "Suit yourself. You can keep the room." He moved outside, leaving the door open. He made it to the steps before he checked to see if she was behind him. She was. He ignored her as he continued down the stairs and through the galley. He planned to stop at the admin cube to say goodbye but could see that the lights were out, and the door was left open.

Stepping closer, it was apparent the space had been evacuated. Things were happening faster than he thought they would. He turned and waved the girl ahead of him as they traveled into the motor pool building, where more troops were running in all directions. At the corner of the large garage, under halogen lighting, the Beast sat alone with the back ramp dropped. Marines were in a bay next to it, strapping gear to the top of an armored Humvee. As Luke approached his Mine Resistant Ambush Protected (MRAP) vehicle, he expected to be confronted, but the men ignored him, consumed with their own work.

He moved around the large, black-painted vehicle and to the back ramp. He removed his pack and tossed it into the troop compartment then waved his fingers at the girl, indicating her bag. She hesitated before unslinging it and stuck it out toward him. He took it and did the same, tossing it into the crew compartment.

"Hey, careful with that."

Luke shook his head and looked at her then pointed to a stack of boxes along a far wall. Marines were moving with purpose over the garage, hardly noticing them. "Make yourself useful. Go to that stack of boxes. It's Meals Ready to Eat; grab as many as you can carry and load them inside."

"They ain't going to just let me steal their stuff," she said, looking at the Marines working nearby.

"That stack and the water next to it are mission rations. It's not stealing—that's what it's for," he said, looking at her sternly.

The girl looked at him with her jaw open. "Just for anything? You have piles of food like this, and we starve in the survivors' block?"

"Cool story, sister, now do what I said."

Not waiting to see if she was following his instruction, he moved to the cab of the vehicle and unlatched the door. He flipped on the power and watched the dash lights and gauges come to life. The tank was topped off. He powered it back down and moved to the rear deck. The six 5-gallon jerry cans were all full.

Things were all prepped and ready to go, the same as he'd left the Beast over a week ago when he backed it into this bay. He looked at his watch—not even midnight. They would have a long wait before Weaver and his men joined them.

There was a rumbling in the bay beside him, and the armored Humvee began to roll forward, toward the main doors. He looked in the direction of the main garage bay and saw groups of armed men gathering near the overhead doors. He spotted Master Gunnery Sergeant Allen "Gus" Gustafson carrying a large duffel bag. He was the grizzled, senior enlisted man of the camp, and from what Luke had heard, the man was essentially leading the camp's defenses.

Before Luke could duck and turn away, he'd caught Gus' attention. The older man scowled and knife-handed a row of Marines standing nearby, shouting obscenities that launched the Marines into action. He then turned and stomped directly in Luke's direction.

Luke stepped away from the MRAP. He could see Kate returning from the supply stack with her arms clumsily wrapped around a box of MREs. She disappeared up the back ramp of the MRAP, and he turned to follow her, trying to avoid a confrontation with Gus. Before Luke could get up the ramp, he heard the old man behind him.

"Are you going somewhere?"

Luke didn't turn around. "Just routine maintenance. Truck needs to be ready, you know."

Kate stepped out of the crew compartment and onto the ramp. Her hands on her hips, she said, "I loaded three cases—how long are we going to be gone?"

Gus looked at the girl, his face stone hard then turned back to Luke and scowled. "Not going anywhere, huh?"

Luke waved his hand for the girl to get back inside then dropped his arms and turned toward the senior Marine. He shook his head. "Nope, but if I was... would you let me?"

Rubbing his clean-shaven chin with his right hand, Gus looked down at his boots and dropped the large duffel bag at Luke's feet. "Nothing I can do to stop you. Colonel says all you cops are free to do what you want. We're running a base camp here, not a prison. Folks are welcome to leave with whatever it was they arrived with. The vehicle is yours, along with what you brought in with you—nothing more, nothing less. So no, I wouldn't stop you."

Luke smiled. He knew Gus was ignoring the obvious fact about the MREs he'd just seen the girl load. They weren't part of the *anything he came in with*. He began to speak but before he could, Gus cut him off. "Does this trip have anything to do with that Sergeant Gyles friend of yours?"

"Gyles? Why? Something I should know?"

"It's a small camp. Not much you can keep a secret, including that girl you're keeping in your room." Gus scoffed a chuckle when he saw Luke's jaw drop. "Don't worry about it. I read the report. I'm sure you didn't have any other options." He stepped closer. "I know your friend Gyles hasn't checked in from his AM patrol. I just checked the books; that Sergeant Weaver up there also cleared a team of his men from the mission log. He's had a group draw full kit and ammo in the last hour. You're going out with Weaver, looking for Gyles, aren't you?"

Luke was prepared to lie, but before he could, Gus put up his hand and pointed toward the overhead doors. "You see those boys over by the exit? You know where they're headed to?"

"I heard something about the southern wall."

"See? Nothing is a secret in this damn place." Gus laughed and nodded his head. "You know why they're going to the wall and not the gate?" Gus asked. He'd turned now and was watching the Marines load cans of ammo into the back of the Humvee.

"Because the gates are blocked with infected," Luke said.

Gus turned back and grinned then moved back toward the MRAP and sat on a crate of vehicle parts. He fished a cigar from his pocket and flipped it through his fingers before placing the well-worn tip between his lips. "The infected got us boxed in. The gates are blocked... no way to open them without damaging the gates and letting the infected into the inner perimeter fences."

"You think it'll work, pulling the infected to the south wall?"

Gus shook his head no. "Maybe long enough to get

a few trucks out. We have drone footage, but it's always delayed because of the comms outage. They can only fly on pre-programmed routes, and we must download the footage when they return. But we do know there are a lot of them out there, and more on the way. The most recent video shows a column stretching all the way back to the Capital."

"So you're not evacuating?" Luke asked. "Then what is this?"

"It's Camp Alamo, son. We need to stop them here, and there's only one thing that can stop them, and that's something we don't got."

"What is it you need?"

"Air support." Gus's face grew hard and his eyes locked on Luke.

"Why are you looking at me like that? I can't fly."

"Because I know there is a fighter attack squadron still in operation. I know they still have birds, fuel, and plenty of ordnance."

"Where?" Luke asked. "Even if there were such a unit still running, by the time we reached them—hell, if we reached them—it would be too late."

Gus grinned and nodded, eyes still locked on Luke's. "But with the radios, we could call in a strike on demand. We could turn this fight around for a while."

"But the radios are down—" Luke stopped when he saw Gus's eyebrows arch, and he shot a grin of his own. "Or maybe someone just doesn't want us talking?"

"Ain't no damn secrets in this camp, are there?"

Gus looked down at his cigar and said "fuck it" before fishing a Zippo from his pocket. He put the flame to the cigar and puffed until a cherry had formed the end.

"Thought the Colonel said no smoking indoors."

Gus sucked in and blew smoke rings toward Luke. "He did, and he'll be pissed when he finds out, but not as pissed as he'll be about what I'm going to tell you. "

"And what's that?" Luke asked.

"I know where this jamming is coming from."

Luke dipped his chin and took a step back to lean against the MRAP, crossing his arms across his chest. "Well, talk is, the Colonel has communications with Fort Stewart now. So what's the problem?"

"Problem is someone is censoring us. Someone is controlling when we can and cannot talk, and who we talk to. They're holding back all the resources and fire power. We're supposed to be fighting a war to save the damn country, but some pencil breaker in a bunker out west is holding everything back," Gus said, the pitch in his voice turning angry. "They're using everything to save their own asses while our people die out there on the streets."

Luke bit at his lower lip. "What do you need me to do, Master Guns?"

"I can't release any Marines. We need everything we've got for the camp's defense."

"I'm listening," Luke said.

"I know you and your battle buddies are already up to something. I know that Sergeant Gyles pal of yours is already out there doing his own thing." Gus turned and looked behind him then back to Luke. "In a couple hours, we're going to open the doors up and attempt to get vehicles outside the wire to make some noise. When that happens, I want your crew moving with them. My men are going to turn east and try to draw away the hordes."

"You're just going to let us go after Gyles?" Luke asked. "You just said you can't spare anyone."

Gus shook his head. "No, *I'm not letting you do anything.* As far as anyone else is concerned, you are part of the defense plan." He looked Luke in the eye and grinned. "But that's not what's going to happen. I want you to disappear, and then find this jamming station and shut it down."

Luke grimaced. "And why would we be down for that? Like you said, we already have plans."

"Cause you do this for me, once it is done, you're free to do whatever you want. Go save your buddy, head to Vegas and find a hooker with a pulse, I don't care. You refuse, I'll just make sure none of your crew ever leaves the wire again. This is your chance to get out safely. Just try leaving on your own with those things pressed against the gate."

"Just find the tower and shut it down?" Luke said. "I take it the Colonel isn't on board with this plan."

Gus shook his head side to side. He handed Luke a scrap of a map. "Don't worry about the Colonel. Our intel guys have pinpointed the source of the jamming. I want you to find it and kill it. It's time to lift the fog of war so my Devil Dogs can do what they do best. We can rally and get the zoomies dropping snake and nape on those crazy bastards." The old Marine reached out an arm and squeezed Luke's shoulder. "If you can't pull this off, Camp Alamo will fall. We don't have the ammo or the real estate to maneuver. They'll all die."

Luke pursed his lips as he looked at the scrap of paper with eight-digit grid coordinates scrawled across it. "Anything else?"

The old Marine pointed down at the duffel bag at his feet. "It's full of demo charges, everything the Seabees could spare. Don't come back here when you're done." Gus took a long pull on the cigar and exhaled. "You free up the radio, we'll start calling in sorties. As soon as the Air Boys can clear the gates of hell, we'll be bugging out."

The old man shot Luke a last toothy grin. "And besides, the Colonel won't be happy with you going AWOL and destroying government property."

CHAPTER NINE

DAY OF INFECTION, PLUS EIGHTEEN

North of Hayslette, Virginia

Back in the bell tower, Gyles was overlooking the outer grounds of the church. The group from earlier was gone, and he found himself alone with a pair of watch standers who were being very open about ignoring him. The sun was setting in the western sky, and the surrounding city was blanketed in a haze of grey smoke.

The stairwell door behind him clunked open, and he turned to see Lawson exiting, holding a steel mess tray in his hand. Extending the tray toward Gyles, he said, "It ain't much, but you're welcome to it."

Gyles looked at the tray with two slices of bread and some sort of stew. "My men eat?"

Lawson nodded. "They're down there now," he said, passing the tray to Gyles.

The old man walked past him and moved to the

tower railing. "Noticed you didn't waste any time getting away from the families down there. You have one of your own?"

Gyles turned his head to the side and shook his head no. He moved his back against the wall, holding the tray. "I'm not here to make friends." He pointed his chin toward the Primals in the street below. "Besides, why miss out on this view?"

"When was the last time you spent a night in the city, Sergeant?"

Stuffing a hunk of bread covered in stew into his mouth, Gyles shrugged. "You can call me Gyles, or Robert, if you'd like."

Grinning, the old man nodded and asked the question again.

"The city? Or any city?" Gyles answered before he sighed and looked around him. "No, this isn't something we make a habit of." He reached for his canteen and chugged water. "Patrols leave in the morning, and we try to get back before sundown. Usually it works out that way. We get a target in the brief, we move to it, take what we can, and move back."

"So why was today different?" Lawson asked.

Gyles shook his head. "To be honest, I don't really know. After seeing all those dead inside the market, something was tearing at me. Something telling me there was more we could be doing. I just had a hunch someone was still alive out here. It can't all be gone."

"Then you haven't seen it."

"Seen what?" Gyles asked, his curiosity piqued.

"Nighttime is when the infected get active," Lawson said. "But it's also when the survivors talk."

"What do you mean talk?"

"There are people out there. A lot of them. I imagine there are people like this all over the country, holed up, just looking for help, and they would ask for it too, if the radios worked."

"We've been out every day, we've found almost nobody in two weeks."

"Because you were always looking in the daylight." Lawson smiled, watching the last of the sun drop below the horizon. "Just wait and see."

Gyles set the now nearly empty mess tray on a small table and stepped closer to the railing. In the distance, he began to see the twinkling of lights. A few at first, then there were several from rooftops all over the city. "Is that Morse code?" he asked.

Lawson shrugged. "It's possible; nobody here knows how to read it very well. It seems pretty random. Some, we know, is S.O.S, but a lot is just random. It's survivors letting others know they are still there."

"Why don't they get out? You said the National Guard was set up here, why didn't they leave?"

The old man moved away from the railing and pulled up a chair, dropping into it. "At first, there were no evacuations. They wanted everyone to lock down tight. Highways were closed, you all were bombing them and killing anything that violated the curfews. It wasn't safe to travel—get infected or have the military kill you."

Gyles frowned at the comment. "I know it happened, but it wasn't anything to do with me."

Lawson nodded. "Same difference though. The government made it clear that they didn't want us traveling. The Army set up barricades to keep the infected out and us in. They killed off everything they could inside the city then started dropping off FEMA kits to survivors. You know, food, water, things like that. They went door-to-door, delivering them. They came with these little instruction cards, telling us to stay indoors, shelter in place, to turn in our sick neighbors. Stuff like that.

"For a minute, it seemed like things would get better. We had no way to find out what was going on. Radio and TV was out, phones dead. The only news we had came from those National Guard troopers. But still, it felt like order was being restored."

The old man paused and looked up into the night sky. "Sure, the power was out, but nobody was going hungry. They tried hard to make sure everyone that wanted food kits had at least thirty days of food. Hell, my pantry was fuller than it had ever been."

"Did they get supplies to everyone?"

Lawson laughed and reached into a back pocket. Removing a flask, he unscrewed the cap and took a swig before passing it to Gyles. "Nah... that operation lasted a whole three, maybe four days. We got a couple of their kits. Some FEMA officer and civilian doctor was telling us to lock our doors and stay put, promised if an evacuation came, that they would move us."

"I take it that didn't happen?" Gyles asked, taking a sip and passing back the flask.

The old man shook his head. "No, it didn't, but this sergeant, he waited until everyone had moved outside then warned us. He said that the security perimeter was shrinking by the day. The infected were close to breaking through, and that there was no plan to evacuate anyone, not even the military. He said we would be better off getting closer to the city center if we could. That's why we came here."

"Was it that easy? Just get in the car and drive away?" Gyles asked with his brow raised.

Lawson shrugged. "Mostly, but I knew we had to move. It just felt right, I guess. Most places inside the perimeter were already a ghost town. All the activity and fighting was out on the edges. People in the city had their doors locked and windows boarded up. With the food drops, there was no reason to go outside. I already had the truck in the garage, so we just loaded it.

"Then just before noon, on I think it was the fifth day, we rolled out. The wife had heard that some of the other fellas from the VFW were holing up at the church so that's what we did. It's always comfortable being around folks you're familiar with."

"That's when you ran into Sherman?" Gyles asked.

Taking another sip from the flask, he exhaled and nodded. "Yes sir. Zeke and Sherman were already here with their families and some of the other boys. Sherman told us how he'd found the church overrun and Andre barricaded downstairs. They did some serious room clearing to get them all out. Zeke was a tunnel rat in Nam though. I'm sure he made easy work of clearing the basement. And that old fella, Sherman, don't look like much, but you'd want no better friend in a fight."

Gyles nodded his head. The flask was offered, and he accepted it. "I still don't understand why you all stayed. If the place was overrun and the city falling, why didn't you all just bail with the Guard soldiers, go to the FEMA camps with the rest of them?"

Laughing, Lawson said, "Place wasn't truly over-run. Before Sherman got here, Andre was letting any scratched or infected person through them doors. He had the place opened to everyone. No security, every door unlocked. After Sherman got here and cleared it out, he made this place a fortress. We were feeling pretty good about it, especially with the Guard making regular supply runs and keeping the infected blocked up at the railroad crossing."

Gyles thought about the answer, and it seemed reasonable, considering these folks were no worse off than his own men at Camp Alamo. They had secure walls and food, same as they did. At least until the infected showed up, and then he knew how it would end.

He stopped thinking and looked seriously at the old man. "Listen, Lawson, I don't know what experience you have with these things, but when they mass up like they are doing right now, they'll come at these walls hard. They'll pile up until they spill right on top of you, then they'll breach every locked door you have and kill every man, woman, and child hiding inside."

"You sound like you're speaking from experience, son," Lawson said, taking the flask back.

Gyles pursed his lips. He looked down at his boots and sighed. "I tried to hold off with a group, not much unlike this one. We were locked in tight, had high fencing, armored vehicles, and a platoon of heavily armed men."

"Don't sound too bad."

"We lasted less than an hour once they hit the walls in force," Gyles said, looking away. "The fences fell like they were made of foil. I won't go through that again. The only way to survive the hordes is to stay ahead of them. I'm giving you all an option. In the morning, we're leaving. You all can come with us or stay here to die."

"We don't have any vehicles. How the hell are we supposed to get out? You going to strap all those people to the roof of your vehicle?"

Gyles shook his head. "We'll have to figure something out. We can't stay."

"So, you're just going to leave and go out there with the street full of demons. You think nothing's going to happen?" Lawson protested. "How do you expect to get out without them getting in?"

Gyles shook his head. "Let me worry about that. My people are fine with fighting them on the streets, but I won't die a caged rat. And I won't ask my men to do that again." He stopped and looked back down at the mob in the street. "If it comes to it, we'll go out and make a hell of a lot of noise and clear a path for you."

Lawson shook his head again. "I'm really not sure how many ways I can break this down for you. We don't have vehicles. We're stuck here, son."

"And I have to make sure you understand. If we stay, we die," Gyles said, his eyes still on the mob below.

He swept his head along the wall and could see that the infected now had them surrounded. The streets to the north, east, and west were all full. The only exception was a small stretch of alley behind the garage buildings in the back. He pointed down at the street below them and clenched his jaw, trying to hold back his anger.

"It might be too late, anyway. As soon as the sun goes down, they are going to hit us. By morning, that inner yard will have as many in it as there are outside. If we're lucky, they won't break through—but most likely, they will. They will corner everyone. I'm talking literal corners as they rip children from mothers' arms. Then there will be nothing left but individual survival."

Lawson stood from his chair and went to the railing, looking down toward the main gate. Unshaken from the soldier's speech, he kept his eyes on the gate below as he spoke in a low steady voice. "Are you trying to scare me, son? You think I haven't seen shit in the last three weeks?" He stopped and turned to face Gyles. The other men on the deck took notice of the commotion and turned in to face the pair. "I need you to know, Sergeant, there is no way out for us. We don't have a bus ... we don't have cars. Do you expect us to walk?"

A cracking voice from the shadows sounded off. "Maybe Joe could help."

Gyles turned back. A frail red-haired boy stood with his arms cradling a lever action 30-30 with a cedar stained stock. The kid was dressed in canvas pants and wore a flannel shirt two sizes too big, with a leather bandoleer of brass across his chest. He paused and looked down, embarrassed by Gyles's glare. He gulped then said again, "I said maybe Joe can help."

"Who is Joe?" Gyles asked.

Lawson waved his hand. "He's a fool; don't waste your time on this nonsense."

The boy shook his head rapidly. "No sir, it ain't nonsense. Mister Joe Hansen, he's got a truck. He come in two days ago on foot, but he said he has got an eighteen-wheeler just a few blocks away." The kid walked around the other side of the tower and pointed into the distance. In the faint light, less than three blocks away, Gyles could make out the shape of what was once a police roadblock. Cars were backed up and pressed tightly together for at least fifty feet, then behind it all was a semi-truck sitting all alone in the center of the street.

"Right there. He says it's his truck. Joe said he saw one of our signs and had tried to make it to the church, when he ran into the roadblock. He said they saw him and started after him. Instead of backing out, he ditched the truck and made a run for it.

"But look at that trailer—it would be enough to get everyone out of here. Sure, it won't be comfortable, but it will get us out. We could leave if we got that truck."

Gyles looked at Lawson. "Where is this Joe?"

Lawson gritted his teeth. "The guy is a loon. He came in here a few days ago on foot and in his underwear, covered head to toe in scratches."

Gyles raised his eyebrows. "Scratches? How'd he keep from getting infected?"

Lawson laughed. "Oh, he says the scratches weren't from the crazies, said he got them crawling through brush and brambles. Claims he ran through them to keep the infected from following him."

"If he had a truck, why didn't he just drive that here?"

"Fool said he got hung up in traffic and walked in the rest of the way. Asked us to help him back it out and said he would give us a ride to wherever we wanted to go."

"Then why didn't you take him up on it?"

Lawson shook his head. "Cause, like I said, the guy is nuts. It probably ain't even his truck."

"Well, how long has it been there?" Gyles asked.

"None of the boys can seem to remember, best guess is it appeared the same day Joe showed up."

"So it's probable that it's his truck," Gyles said.

Lawson shrugged. "Maybe. For all I know, he is a homeless vagrant, just looking for a place to hole up;

could have just walked past the truck and came up with a good story."

"Would you have let him in without a story?" Gyles said.

Lawson nodded. "Of course we would have."

"Then he had no reason to lie," Gyles grinned. "I need to talk to this Joe Hansen about the whereabouts of his truck."

CHAPTER TEN

DAY OF INFECTION, PLUS NINETEEN

Camp Alamo, Near Hayslette, Virginia

Just past 02:00, the bay became busy with activity. Luke watched as Marines, armed to the teeth, moved back and forth with ammo cans and cases of supplies. Vehicles were started, exhausts belching black smoke as they pulled into position in a long line just inside the overhead doors. Luke stood nervously outside the cab of the MRAP, tapping his boot. His own vehicle was loaded and ready for departure, all the compartments stuffed with food, ammo, and water. The young girl was in the passenger seat, fast asleep. Luke could hear her snoring from his perch outside.

He had no idea what he was doing or why he was doing it. All of this seemed to suddenly be pushed on him. He had no ties to this girl, no responsibility to her morally or otherwise, yet here he was. And what was he doing, putting his neck out for even more people he had no connection to? Why was it his problem if Gyles wanted to play cowboy and save the world? And even then, if that worked out, he would just be moving on to do something stupid for even more people. He should be trying to get home, back to his own family.

Just like back at Vines. He should have ignored the sheriff's calls for volunteers to report to the station. He should have packed his bags when the news got shady and headed for his kin on the East Coast. What good did it do for him to stay there? He shook his head and whispered, "They all died, anyway." At the same time, Luke couldn't give up hope. *No, they didn't all die. Some of them got out.*

He watched as Marines gathered close to the doors for final convoy briefings. Men checking each other's armor, snapping magazines into pockets on tactical vests. "I got my own family. I have a vehicle and food... maybe it's time to find out what happened out there," he mumbled to himself. "To hell with this mess; it's why I got out of the corps in the first place. Time to put me first."

He was about to give in to his own temptations and pull the MRAP into position, without the backup of the soldiers, when he spotted Weaver and three heavily armed men moving down the hallway. Each man was decked out in body armor with heavy packs on their backs. Luke knew they'd gotten the word. This wasn't a short recovery mission; these men were planning on leaving and not coming back.

The soldiers approached the vehicle. Luke knew

each of them. They were familiar faces from their fight out of the George Washington National Forest just two weeks ago. Looking into their determined faces, he forgot all about his notions of abandoning them. He began to relax, being back in the company of friends and men he trusted.

O'Riley, the lean farm boy, Scott, the Philly tough guy, and Sergeant Tucker, who no matter how hard he tried, couldn't shake the Jersey City accent. These were Weaver's boys, the original troops of his first squad. Men who had been to war with the sergeant and back again, they were dedicated to him the same as if he was their own flesh and blood. They moved past Luke and piled into the rear of the truck as if they were struck with boredom, hardly saying a word.

Weaver pulled up by his side and shrugged off his pack. "You get the word? You know what's up, right? What we have planned?"

Luke nodded. "Gus gave me the lowdown; we been suddenly sanctioned by Master Guns to do some dirty laundry. I take it most of the boys aren't aware of what's going on here?"

"Oh, they are *woke* to the cause, brother," Weaver said with a sly smile. "Except we ain't going after that tower like Guns wants us to."

"Then what are we doing?" Luke asked.

"We rescue Sergeant Gyles like we already planned. We get our boy back, and then—if we still have something left in the tank—I'm fine with the tower mission. But either way, we are off the sidelines and back in the fight."

"Hells yes we are, Sergeant," a man yelled from behind Luke. He spun back to look at Sergeant Tucker just before he entered the vehicle, the veins bulging in the black man's neck. "We're tired of being on the sidelines, grocery shopping. Time to get back out there, give me something to kill."

Luke forced a laugh. "Oh, so you're born again hard now, aye, Sergeant Tucker? I seem to remember you nearly shitting yourself in the back of my MRAP a couple weeks ago."

Tucker waved a dismissive hand. "You just drive this beast, that sexy way you do," the man said, turning the corner and climbing the ramp into the back. "Then you can see how hard I am," Tucker shouted, the others bursting into laughter.

The girl, startled awake from the loud voices, turned back toward the cab then looked over the console and into the eyes of Luke standing in the open driver's door. He raised a hand, calming her. "Don't worry about it... these are friends." He looked down at Weaver. "Isn't that right?"

Weaver grinned. "If we weren't friends, I wouldn't have even told you about this mission." He laughed. "I'd a left you with that Puerto Rican gal of yours."

"Hell no," Luke laughed.

"You know the staff are all leaving too, right? They're all bugging out any day now, once they get the all clear." Weaver paused and looked at the young girl in the passenger seat. "We could get another vehicle, if you think that's a better option for you."

"Man, stow that nonsense," Luke spat, shaking his head. "Who else would be dumb enough to give you a ride?" Luke waved his hand, dismissing the suggestion. "Get in. You all are late—the bay doors are about to open, and I suspect stuff will be happening fast after that."

He briefed the men on what he knew of the plan about the misdirection, the objective to lead the infected away so the base defense forces could circle away to the front and allow them and other camp defenders to break away. He also pulled the scrap of paper and passed it back to Weaver. "What do you think? Is that tower even there?"

Weaver unfolded it and looked at the numbers. He reached into a thigh pocket and pulled out a plastic-wrapped tactical map with several routes already outlined in green or red, depending on their conditions. He stared at the paper then back to the map before leaning forward between the seats. "Is this some kind of joke?"

"Am I laughing?" Luke said, looking back at him.

"This is Mount Weather. It's a major installation, not just some radio antenna. Lots of stories about this place. And if the tower is there and operational, it's not likely to just be sitting out in the open, waiting for someone to come knock it down."

Luke smiled and placed the MRAP into gear, joining the other vehicles lined up at the exit doors. "Then let's get our boy and become legends."

"That's what I'm saying!" Tucker bellowed from the back. "We get Gyles first—then if there's time, we head out there and crack skulls, blow some shit up."

Weaver shook his head and stuffed the scrap of paper into his shirt pocket then taped the tactical map to the center console, which would have normally held a large military radio. Instead, there was just a tray with two small portable walkie talkies and a civilian band (CB) radio. He pointed to a town to the northeast on the map that was circled in red grease marker. "Gyles was headed here, that's where we'll try first."

Luke nodded then held up a hand, silencing the men in the back as the overhead doors began to crank up. Lights inside the bay were shut off, and the vehicle headlights switched to blackout drive. Engines revved, and men inside the building took up fighting positions around the top perimeter of the bay, up on the overhead catwalks.

Before anyone could speak, a machine gun opened fire in a roof turret then tracer fire rained down from the catwalks above. The entire garage space was lit with a dizzying strobe of muzzle flashes and tracer fire. As the doors continued to crank open, streams of infected raced through the bottom. The bodies were torn apart as they crossed paths with the gunfire. Still, the doors kept opening, and the infected continued to swarm. Kate began frantically screaming in the passenger seat, seeing the infected fill the garage and run directly at the MRAP.

Luke looked back over his shoulder at Weaver. Without having to speak the order, the man reached up and snatched the girl back into the crew compartment with one arm. Before the heavy MRAP rolled forward, Weaver was seated up front. Luke followed close to the lined-up vehicles. One, two, three, four passed through the open bay, the only light being the menacing strobes of muzzle flashes. Luke gripped the wheel as he approached the opening, waiting for his turn in the breach.

On the outside, Luke spotted two of the heavy Seabee dozers covered in plate steel with large spotlights shining down on the packs of infected. He couldn't see the operators through the clumps of infected grabbing onto the sides of the dozer as it spun left and right, snagging Primals and pulling them down into the tracks, throwing off unrecognizable mush from the rear treads.

The overhead door screeched at the top and began to roll down as Luke approached it. Suddenly, he realized his eyes had been focused on the outside. He looked back at the vehicle bay—and wished he hadn't. The garage around them was a nightmare of bloodied and screaming bodies. But as bad as it was inside, it was worse beyond the doors.

"Holy gates of hell, what are we doing out here?" Weaver said.

"You've been out of the wire before... I take it this is different."

Weaver shook his head and placed his palms on the dash to his front. "I've seen nothing like this, brother. I heard the horde had us surrounded, but holy hell—nothing like this when we came back this afternoon."

Luke willed the MRAP forward, mentally gluing himself to the armored Humvee to his front. Fire pots of diesel exploded off to their right, casting a bright glow across the night sky. Bits of sticky flame and bodies fell from the sky, striking the armored vehicles in the convoy. Then the wall to the right of them erupted in gunfire, with even more riflemen joining the fight from the rooftops of the complex. He dared a look over his left shoulder and could see Marines standing shoulder to shoulder firing into the mobs of infected, tracers zipping all around them.

A shirtless infected man climbed onto the hood of the MRAP and looked inside, his mouth grotesquely wide, screaming at the occupants. Rounds pinged off the sides of the MRAP, and the man's chest and head exploded, the body rolling off the side. The vehicles in the convoy went boot heavy, picking up speed as they lurched forward. As Luke crunched over the masses of bodies, the wheel shuddered in his hands. The convoy wended down a raised road then turned, headed around the perimeter road that circled the factory. Luke looked across at Weaver. "This is it; this is the distraction."

Luke slammed down the pedal and cut the wheel

hard into the wall of infected on their left, driving through a sea of bodies. Screams and grinding from under the wheels shuddered through the armor until the wheels finally found purchase on a paved road. Luke leaned in, his face against the glass, squinting to see out as he white knuckled the wheel, fighting through the mob. Slowly, as he gained separation on the camp, the hordes thinned out and eventually turned to nothing.

Luke stopped the MRAP and pushed back into the seat, his body still shaking. His clothing was soaked with sweat; he was panting and thirsty. He turned his head and stared into the large rearview mirror on the driver's side that somehow managed to stay attached during the escape. Behind them, Camp Alamo was blanketed in a storm of explosive flashes and tracer fire.

"They're dead if we can't stop the jamming," he said without turning his head. "If they don't get help, they'll all die."

"Then let's go get Sergeant Gyles and get it done," Tucker said quietly from the back.

Luke shook his head, not speaking, his eyes still locked on the mirror as he watched the base fighting for its life. He knew what had to be done, even if he didn't want to say it out loud.

Weaver pulled the scrap of paper from his shirt pocket and compared it with the tactical map taped to the console. Using a grease pencil, the soldier circled a new destination. "I'm sure Gyles will be okay for a bit longer." He pointed his hand to the west. "Let's knock out this tower, boys. The Marines need us to bail them out."

CHAPTER ELEVEN

DAY OF INFECTION, PLUS NINETEEN

North of Hayslette, Virginia

Gyles walked through the dark sanctuary. Pews had been moved to the sides and small family spaces were formed around a central aisle. He spotted his own men in a corner, Mega and Culver passed out as Kenny sipped from a canteen cup. All around the room, parents stood watch over sleeping children. The people held all sorts of weapons, from axe handles to single-barrel shotguns. Even though far past midnight, some still worked the meager camp kitchen, heating pots of coffee. He investigated the weary faces then yawned, beginning to feel his own fatigue.

"How long since you've slept, Sergeant?" Zeke whispered.

Gyles looked beside him at the elderly man in the olive-green Army field jacket. He shrugged. "Real sleep? I don't know... two, maybe three weeks—however long ago this shit started."

"You should sleep then. Go find you a spot at the end down there. You can talk to Joe in the morning, he isn't going anywhere," Zeke said.

"It can't wait," Gyles answered, catching a glare from a woman sitting on a stool, cradling a baby. She held a finger to her lips, hushing them. Zeke smiled at her and pointed off to a far wall lined with chairs, directing the sergeant away from the crowd.

Nodding, Gyles continued to make his way through the sanctuary, stopping near the tall wooden doors that were now secured and locked. He found an empty chair along a back wall and sat heavily. Zeke moved close and stopped beside him, his eyes studying the curled up and sleeping bodies inside the church. He pointed to a corner of the sanctuary. "I think I see Joe. Why don't you wait here, and I'll bring him to you."

Sighing and rubbing an arm across his forehead, Gyles nodded his approval then took a stool and put his feet up before leaning back against the wall. The old man was right; he did need to sleep. The Reaper Platoon had been on the go for at least twenty-four hours, and he didn't even know what sleep they'd had prior to that. He let his body shut down; his shoulders slumped while he kept his eyes open and mind fixed on the room to his front. He watched as Zeke wound his way through the sleeping bodies on the floor of the church.

Near the front of the room, the old man stopped and shined a flashlight over a row of sleeping bags. A husky man sat up and shielded his eyes from the light. Zeke pointed back toward Gyles, and the groggy man dipped his chin. He crawled from the bag and stood, pulling on a pair of trousers. A door slammed on the opposite side of the room, and Gyles watched as an armed man ran along the outside wall toward another door that Gyles knew led to the keep below them.

When he looked back to his front, Zeke was standing there with the big, husky man. He wore canvas pants and a heavy blue work shirt with a red fanny pack on his hip. But on top of all of that, he wore a thick leather belt of .410 shotgun slugs over his shoulder. Gyles ignored the stranger for the moment and pointed to the door the armed man had moved through. "Something going on?" he whispered to Zeke.

Zeke nodded. "Yeah, I saw it too. Boys are getting twitchy tonight with the infected so close. We haven't seen them like this before. Always in the streets, but never piled up against the gates."

"Maybe you haven't, but I've seen plenty," the husky man interrupted. "You all need to think about leaving, and do it soon."

Scratching his chin, Gyles examined the man. He certainly looked the type of a truck driver, that is if truckers had a type. "This is Hansen, I take it?"

"They just call me Joe here; Joe will do just fine, if you don't mind."

Gyles smiled. "I hear you've got a truck, Joe."

The man shook his head no. "I *had* a truck. I left it out there when I got hung up at a roadblock. Things were about to start chewing on my ass, so I ran. But like I been telling these folks, all I need is some help moving parked cars out of the way, and we could be on the road again. Most of the road to the church is clear past the roadblock."

"Clear of infected?" Gyles asked.

"You trying to be funny, soldier boy? Hell no, it's not clear of infected," Joe gasped. "There's lots of them, but the truck doesn't mind running them down, either."

Gyles tightened his brow. He had begun to speak, when he saw the small door from the keep open again. The armed man was back and headed toward the tower stairs, this time with Lawson and Sherman close in tow. Gyles looked at Zeke again. "Is this something I need to be worried about?"

Zeke had his eyes focused on the trio as they entered the stairway and closed the door behind them. Shortly after that, gunshots echoed from high above them, and what had been dull moans outside erupted into ravenous screams and howls. Zeke's head snapped back to Gyles. "Yeah, you need to be worried."

The soldier sprang to his feet. Looking across the space, he could see his men were up and looking for him, Mega cradling the machine gun with Culver and Kenny flanking him. Gyles raised a hand and circled it over his head, calling them in. The men immediately took notice and moved in his direction. He turned back to the trucker. "You got a shotgun to go with those .410 rounds, Joe?"

The man shook his head no. He reached into the fanny pack around his waist and retrieved a Judge revolver. "Got this though."

Moving in from the back, Mega pointed and laughed. "Is that a fanny pack?"

Joe looked down at his hip, placing the Judge revolver back into the pocket and zipping it shut. The trucker shook his head. "No, this is a holster."

Mega laughed and walked away, saying, "Bro, you're sick. That's a fanny pack, and you know it."

Gyles waved the big soldier off then pointed back toward where Joe had been sleeping. "You got gear you need, I suggest you go grab it."

"Everything I own is out there in that truck," the man said in a voice that barely elicited interest.

At that time, Mega and the others closed in. Mega went to speak, when Gyles held up his palm. "Listen, if this is what I think it is, we're about to be hit hard. And we know from Vines that we got one chance, and that is to get the hell out of here before they get in."

"I told you, mister, my truck is hung up blocks from here."

Nodding, Gyles pointed at Kenny. "I saw the truck from the tower. I can get you there, and we just happen to have an Uber driver that's more than willing to guide us back."

"I am?" Kenny said.

"Yeah, that's what scouts do, right? Find a path?" Gyles said, winking.

Kenny looked back at the others then nodded his head nervously. "Take me to where you left the truck, and I'll get us there and back no problem."

"Good," Gyles said. "But we will need to move fast. If the yard hasn't already fallen, it soon will."

Joe shook his head and took a step back. "Even if we do get my truck, what good will that do us here? Like I said, the road is blocked. How you going to clear it in the dark with all of them things out there?"

Gyles bit his lip. "Just take Kenny to the truck, he'll navigate us back here."

"How? I been telling you, there's a roadblock," Joe said.

Turning and looking back at the families, now awake, Gyles ignored the trucker's concerns. He faced his team. "Have your weapons ready to go, but I have a feeling we're going to have to be quiet on this one, moving on foot and staying in the shadows. If we are spotted, we run and gun. Are you all up for that?"

Culver shook his head. "I don't like it, Sergeant, but sounds like we're out of options."

The gunfire from above quickened in its pace, dozens of rifles all firing at the same time. The moans began to spread to the left side of the church, the sound beating against the cracks of the gunfire.

Gyles looked at Zeke. "Can you get us into the yard? We need to get going."

Zeke shook his head. "I need to talk to Sherman first; he won't like you leaving."

"We aren't leaving, dammit; we're securing transportation to get us all the hell away from here." He pointed his finger in the old man's chest. "You need to get us out of here and make sure these people are ready to go when we get back—now help us save all your asses."

Gyles pulled the handheld radio from his collar and handed it off to Zeke. "Give this to Sherman. It doesn't have range for shit, but when we return, I'll call you. You'll need to tell us where to park that truck." He stopped and looked at Joe. "And you better be able to get it back here." He spun on his feet and moved to the back doors. "Come on, boys, we've got work to do."

He marched off, not looking back. He knew the others would be close. That was the way his troops were trained. They hated the shit just as much as he did, but they all did their part. They protested, called it like it was, then moved on and sucked it up. Walking through the crowd, he could see the people were panicked, stuffing belongings into backpacks. Men gathered rifles and melee weapons. Gyles clenched his jaw, trying to block out the nightmare of Vines that was playing on repeat through his head. Every child he saw in the church reminded him of a baby at Vines. He clenched his teeth and pushed on. He shook his head, knowing the people in here wouldn't last two minutes if the infected got inside.

He reached the heavy double doors and waited

while Zeke ordered them open. Men with nervous expressions pressed in and worked a lock. One man apprehensively pulled the door inward. Gyles waited for a crack wide enough to fit his body then stepped through into the musty hallway, headed for the back entrance. At the rear door, he paused again and waited for his men to stack up behind him. Zeke moved around them and used a skeleton key attached to a string around his neck to unlock the door. He looked at the soldiers then back to Gyles. "Why not take the Hummer?"

Gyles shook his head. "It's too loud. The horde would just block us in and swarm the yard as we tried to get out. We need to do this quiet or not at all."

Zeke grimaced and reached into his field jacket pocket. He pulled a key ring out and handed it to Gyles. "Go through the garage. There is a back door that exits onto the street. You can get into an alley from there and the breakaway. If the path is clear, we can use the same door to get everyone out."

Gyles clenched his teeth and accepted the key ring. He then looked down at the doorknob and dipped his chin. They were ready to move. He looked back at the team and let the rifle hang from its sling. He drew a long fighting knife and watched as the others did the same. "We stay quiet as long as we can. Joe, you stay inside of us. Don't do anything stupid. You understand?"

The big man nodded then put the Judge revolver

back into the fanny pack, replacing it with a shortened bowie knife. "Just get me back to my truck."

"Okay, tough guy," Gyles said, grinning.

Zeke turned the door and slowly let it swing out. To Gyles's relief, the yard was still clear, but the screams of the infected were amplified now that they were down inside the walls. Gyles stepped out and down the stairs, posting up on the sidewalk as he waited for the others to line up behind him. As soon as he felt the tap on his shoulder from Culver, he moved out at a crouch, heading directly toward the side door of the garage. He had the key ring in his hand as soon as he arrived. He heard the clicking of gear as his men moved into position to cover his work. The ring only had two keys, and the first choice was wrong. On the second key, the lock slid into position and turned freely.

He let the door glide open and stood to the side as his men moved in. Keeping his back to the door, he closed it but left it unlocked. He didn't know if Zeke had a second key and didn't want them locked out when it was time to go.

Gyles paused, holding his breath and looking around the space while his eyes adjusted to the darkness. The only light came from a tiny skylight in the ceiling, bleeding in the faintest amount of moonlight. Aside from some gardening tools hanging on the walls, the room was empty. Tire marks on the floor revealed where a pair of vehicles once sat. He moved slowly around the perimeter of the building, finding the back door. He let his hand survey the door in the dark. There was a dead bolt at the top, but the door handle itself had no lock.

Gyles stepped off to the side and looked at Kenny, pointing to the left. Then to Culver and Mega, indicating the right. When he pulled the door in, the men moved in concert. Silently, Kenny slipped out with Joe close behind him, moving to the left, Mega and Culver out and to the right. Gyles followed the team into an alley and shut the door behind him. He checked the key ring and found that the second key fit the bolt lock, so he turned and secured the garage door.

There was some light in the alley, allowing him to see both ends. Behind them to the right on the street that they'd originally approached the church on, he could see moving shadows. To his front to the west, the infected were moving past the alley entrance, presumably to the north, toward the gunfire and the main gate of the church. *As long as they keep moving into the line of fire, they have a chance at holding them off,* he thought. He shook his head, remembering the Vine armory. Any victory will be short-lived. The Primals would hit the gate at first but soon adapt, and eventually hit all sides at once. They needed to hurry.

Kenny was exchanging whispers with Joe, who was pointing in some far-off direction. Gyles let them finish the conversation then waited for Kenny to look back at him. He gave the scout a thumbs up and the team stepped off together, keeping their bodies hidden in the shadow of the wall. Moving slow, they crept along at a crouch, stopping often to listen. Beyond the church, the wall ended, and the alley opened to fenced-in backyards.

Gyles halted the group and surveyed the empty spaces ahead. It was a residential neighborhood. He could see over fences to finely crafted patios and well-kept homes. Grass was long and uncut, showing the time since the infection caused the normal functions of the world to stop. The humidity of late to mid-summer would have the grass growing inches a day. He could see in the dim light a kitchen window. The glass was broken, and the curtains moved faintly in the breeze. He looked down at the glowing dial on his watch then back at Kenny. He moved them out.

At the corner, Gyles held Kenny and Joe back as he slowly approached with Culver. Mega cut the distance and readied his machine gun in case they had to bug out in a hurry. Gyles squatted and advanced to the corner at a near crawl, a split rail fence the only thing providing cover. He moved into the tall grass and pointed toward a tall oak tree, where Culver quickly took up a position. Gyles drew closer to the intersection and looked left and right. A group of Primals had recently passed by, and the next group was still too far away to count their numbers. He readied his legs for a sprint, when Culver's palm shot up in the air, halting him.

Gyles froze and watched as the younger soldier got small, pressing into the base of the tree, trying to disappear. Gyles followed his lead and pressed himself to the ground and slowly moved toward him. Only feet away, he leopard crawled, closing the distance. Culver looked back at him; his face was stone hard. He put a finger to his eye then pointed it to the opposite corner. Gyles strained and tried to focus his eyes in the low light.

It took time to see it, then they moved. A pair of men. They stood still, their heads hardly moving side to side, their eyes searching the street. Before Gyles could speak, he heard footsteps coming from the south. He pushed back and looked to his right. Another group was approaching. "Damn," he whispered.

"What do we do?" Culver asked.

Gyles held his breath then whispered, "Hold tight. We don't move, and they won't see us." He looked back over his shoulder; the rest of his team had disappeared, already taking cover in the shadows. The sounds of shuffling feet grew louder, joined with heavy breathing and grunting, as the group drew closer. Gyles blocked them out and put his focus back on the two figures on the opposite corner. Their bodies shifted slightly to see the approaching mass, then they turned back toward the fighting at the church.

The group moved by, staggering along. Some walked as calmly as if they were on a Sunday stroll, others dragged along broken and damaged limbs. Even in the low light, Gyles could spot wounds and injuries that should have made the things immobile or, at least, bedridden with pain. He counted twenty before the entire group had passed. When he looked back at the far corner, the pair was gone. He lifted back up and pressed in close to Culver. "Did you see where they went?"

"They joined the group and moved north."

Gyles looked back at the spot where the pair had been. He swept the vegetation and the corners then nodded. "I'll cross first. When I give the signal, send the rest."

"Got it, Sergeant," Culver responded.

Gyles took a last look then unslung his rifle, holding it in his left hand, and sheathed his fighting knife into the carrier across his chest. He exhaled then stepped off heavy, running across the street, every foot-fall seeming to echo like a sledgehammer crushing stone. He could hear every jingle and jangle of his equipment, sure the mob would turn and run at him before he reached the far side, and then he was there. He stopped at the side of a parked sedan before dropping to his heels in a squat and pressing his back against the car.

Taking only a moment to catch his breath, he lifted back up and surveyed the space. This side of the alley appeared the same as the one they'd just left—a narrow, single lane dividing backyards in the residential block. He had his back to one home, looking across to another. Gyles looked back, seeing Culver pressed against the tree. Mega, Kenny, and Joe had moved up, readying for their own move across the danger area. Gyles prepared to give the signal, when he heard a low, guttural growl.

CHAPTER TWELVE

DAY OF INFECTION, PLUS NINETEEN

East of Paris, Virginia

Luke eased off the throttle and let the MRAP settle in the middle of the two-lane highway. Looking in the distance, he could see that the road would soon split into four lanes. There was something up there, something that required more than the two-lane county highway they'd been traveling on. Far ahead on the right side of the road was a silent, white farmhouse with barns, outbuildings, and a blacktop driveway. He stared at it for a long time, watching for motion or a flash of white light. Satisfied the place was empty, he let his eyes continue to search the surrounding terrain until stopping on the asphalt to the immediate front of the vehicle. He checked the rearview mirror then closed his eyes and sighed.

He killed the engine, and for the first time since they'd left the camp, he relaxed his back and shoulders, letting his muscles press against the seat. The vehicle was quiet, absent the snoring soldiers in the back. Even surrounded by monsters and behind enemy lines, the men of the Reaper Platoon knew it was important to sleep when they could.

He reached for a bag between the seats and fetched a bottle of water. As he sipped, Weaver stirred and opened his eyes. The man suddenly snapped awake, startled, trying to remember where he was. Luke had seen men at war awaken this way plenty of times. It was usually best to leave them alone and let them work it out on their own. Each man seemed to have his own process. Weaver's eyes quickly scanned the scenery outside the window then finally settled on Luke. "There a problem? Why did we stop?"

"No problem; I just need a break, eyes are starting to play tricks on me in the dark."

Weaver nodded his head wearily and yawned. "What time is it?"

Luke shrugged. "Either really late or real early, depending on how you look at it. Sun should be up soon."

The sergeant scratched at his chin and whispered, "Okay." Then he turned back to the front, searching the terrain through the bulletproof glass, before looking into the back to see his snoring men.

Luke picked up on the sergeant checking his soldiers and asked, "So where are the rest of them?"

"The rest of who?" Weaver asked.

Luke grinned from the side of his mouth. "The

Reapers. You know we ain't coming back. How you going to just go and leave half your people behind at Camp Alamo?"

Weaver yawned again and shook his head. "Nah... it's not like that. We got everyone. Most of those other guys in the platoon were new to us. Bunch of individuals and bits of other units collected by the Colonel. We've been too busy to really conform." Weaver yawned and stretched. "Gyles has Culver and Mega, the rest of my squad are sleeping in the back. I talked to Sergeant Alverez last night. He's been kind of Gyles's right-hand man lately. Good guy, but he's a Georgia boy, through-and-through. He was more than happy to take what's left of the Reapers back to Fort Stewart."

"So that's that then. We're all on our own," Luke said, taking another swig from the bottle and stuffing it back into his pack.

Weaver turned and looked out of the passenger window. "Hard to say. Knowing Gyles, once we get this mess untangled, he'll want to head south and regroup at Stewart anyway."

Luke shook his head. "Then you would be on your own because the Beast isn't headed south," he said, rubbing the dash. "I'm not exactly sure where I'll go, but it ain't that way."

Weaver grinned and dipped his chin. "You'll get no arguments from me on that." His eyes drifted to the old farmhouse just ahead of them. "Say, where the hell are we, anyhow?"

"Nowhere, as far as I can tell. I haven't seen any

infected in a few miles. Once we drove around that last roadblock, things have even gotten suspiciously clear. I figured this was as a good place to rest as any."

"Roadblock? What roadblock?" Weaver exclaimed.

Luke grinned. "Exactly. It wasn't even worth waking you up for. A long line of jersey barriers, some razor wire. But that was it, no patrol cars, no people."

"No Primals? Not even dead ones?" Weaver asked.

Luke shook his head. "Nothing. They had a small lane cut through it, looked like maybe there was a gate once, but they were all gone so I drove right through it."

"So what's ahead then? What am I looking at?"

Luke pointed at the map. "According to your route, we've got less than ten miles left. If this Mount Weather is everything they say it is" —he stopped and checked the windows again before continuing— "then I'm not sure we should be rolling up on it in the dark. Clear or not, people might be trigger happy."

Weaver stretched and focused on the road ahead. There was a small green sign that said Paris 5 Miles just before the large farm complex. He pointed at it and said, "Unless you know where we can find a waffle house, let's go check that place out then hole up until daylight."

"Could be infected inside," Luke said, his brow rising.

Weaver shrugged. "You just said you haven't seen any since before the last roadblock, and besides, we're in the middle of nowhere. Roads are clear." The soldier looked at his watch. "We got some time—maybe we can find some coffee."

Grimacing, Luke restarted the engine and put the big vehicle into gear. He let it slowly roll forward without pressing on the throttle. The slow speed helped him track objects on the side of the road without having to use the headlights. Through the pre-dawn mist, he neared the white farmhouse with clapboard siding they'd spotted earlier. The windows were all intact, curtains drawn. The grass was overgrown, the driveway void of vehicles.

Weaver whispered beside him, "It almost looks like this place has been here, frozen in time. Like the last few weeks of shit went down right around it."

"Been that way for a few miles," Luke said. "It's like the Primals never got up here. Maybe that last roadblock held."

"If it held, then where are the troops that manned it?" Weaver asked, his eyes fixed on the farm.

"Good question."

He guided the vehicle to the shoulder and rolled past the driveway before stopping, then slowly backed into the driveway. If they did find trouble, he wanted to be able to leave in a hurry. He situated the big MRAP at a slight angle and cut the engine. With everything again silent, he made a fuss of undoing his seatbelt harness, waking up the rest of the crew. The soldiers startled awake with Tucker quickly moving toward the cupola turret.

Weaver looked back into the crew compartment. "Relax, heroes; just a pitstop."

Tucker leaned into the turret windows, scanning. "Where in the hell are we?"

Luke ignored the query, pulled his combat lock, and popped his door open. He stepped out into the damp morning air, blinking his eyes to adjust to the low light. He looked left and right and reached back into the cab, pulling his AR-10 down with him. The air was cold and fresh, the dampness feeling good against his skin. He let his rifle hang at the low ready as he looked back in the direction they'd traveled, staring at the silent road. He listened to the clunk and hum as the back ramp dropped.

Soon, the soldiers were pouring out like they were on a mission. The men fanned to the left and right with weapons up, no sign that the soldiers had been silently asleep just minutes earlier. Luke sighed when he spotted Kate slowly walking down the ramp, following close behind the soldiers. The young girl moved into, then stopped in the middle of, their tight bubble of security. The soldiers, sensing her presence, seemed to tighten up, protecting her.

Luke shook his head. "No, Kate, back in the truck."

She looked back and flipped him the bird, stepping closer to the soldiers standing in the dew-covered grass. When she was next to Tucker, she took a knee and hid in the sergeant's shadow. In no mood to argue, Luke ignored the gesture and rounded the front of the MRAP and faced the old farmhouse. Weaver was already there, checking the front door from a distance. His soldiers were slowly moving around the side of the MRAP.

Scott took a knee in the grass with his rifle pointed toward one of the distant barns. The other men lined up close behind each of them and took sectors of their own, with Kate standing near them, holding her slender backpack defiantly. Luke shook his head and smirked then turned back to Weaver.

The man spit in the grass and whispered, "So what? Just like Iraq, we roll up in stack, kick the door, and clear this bitch."

Luke grunted and shook his head no. "This ain't Fallujah, bro. Let's try to be neighborly first."

He stepped off ahead of them toward the big covered front porch. At the top of the stairs was a flimsy screen door. He pulled, and it squeaked open. Behind it was a heavy wooden door with a window at the top. The window was covered with a white linen curtain. Luke rapped his knuckles on the door as he listened to the soldiers rolling up behind him. He waited a beat then knocked again. He held his breath and gripped the knob. It turned and clunked smoothly in his hand. Opening in, he released the knob from his gloved hand and let it swing open with a squeak, revealing the dark room.

Before he could step forward, a shotgun barrel dropped down into his face, followed by a raspy voice. "Something I can help you with, son?"

CHAPTER THIRTEEN

DAY OF INFECTION, PLUS NINETEEN

North of Hayslette, Virginia

Gyles already knew he'd made a tactical error. Before he could stand, the creature was on him, its eyes bulging, jaw extended with canine-like, snapping teeth. The once middle-aged man charged at him, screaming, its arms flailing. Gyles tried to bring his rifle around. Too late—the distance closed by the microsecond. He dropped to his rear and thrust the butt of the rifle upward with all his strength. The end of the stock caught the crazy just above the Adam's apple.

He flinched as he heard the crunch of a broken neck and jaw as the creature's momentum carried it over him and into the car he was kneeling beside. The blood splattered on his cheek, and Gyles frantically wiped it away with his sleeve. He looked at the dark streak on his uniform, still not completely sure how the infection was transferred. He shook his head, pushing away the concern, knowing there was no time to worry about it now. If he didn't fight, he would be dead before some fluid transfer could take place.

He rolled away, still hearing the growl from the Primal. The creature was immobile, its neck broken, eyes continuing to dart left and right while the top of its jaw convulsed. Gyles cursed under his breath and delivered another butt stroke to the creature's temple. This time, the monster went silent. He heard the footfalls of his men closing in beside him. He stepped forward and used the dead monster's shirt to clean the gore from his rifle.

"What the hell happened? Thought you said it was clear," Kenny whispered.

Gyles shook his head. "I think this asshole just ambushed me. He saw us and hid, then waited for me to cross the damn street."

"Bullshit," the big trucker said. "These things are dumb as all get-out; they don't think more than one or two steps ahead. They don't *ambush*."

Kenny held up his hand. "Gyles, you said there were two of them. Where is the other one?"

Before Gyles could answer, there was a roar from blocks behind them. "I think I know." He turned back to Joe. "Get us to your damn truck now."

The big man nodded his head feverishly then took off at a trot with Kenny following close to his side. Gyles stayed put until Mega passed by and pulled him to his feet. They turned and looked behind them, listening to the roar of the infected closing in on them.

This new group wasn't as large as the group attacking the church, but they could tell by the volume that facing them in the open wouldn't be a healthy prospect. Gyles turned to follow the others, and the two men took off at a jog in quick pursuit.

"You know what? That was right," Mega said, his voice at a low roar between breaths as they ran.

Gyles grunted. "Yeah, like I said, he ambushed me. Waited for me to cross then attacked."

Mega swung his head side to side. "Nah, bro, that was a delaying action. The thing came in to sacrifice itself; it slowed us down while the other one went for help."

Gyles could see the group ahead stacking up along the side of a building. He slowed to a walk and turned back, searching the terrain behind them. "Ambush is one thing, but that really goes above and beyond, Mega —that's tactics." He shook his head no. "If that was the case, they could have just screamed when they first saw us. Pointed us out to those on the road and hit us then."

Mega grinned and slapped his weapon. "I don't think so, Sergeant. Think of it this way—those two you saw were just out scouting."

"I'm not tracking, Mega. What the hell are you trying to say?"

Mega shook his head. "You ever hunt wolves, Sergeant? Or better yet, you ever have one hunt your stock?" The big man spun, looking behind him then rushed up to stand beside Gyles. "Back on my grand-pa's ranch out West, they did the same thing. A pair of wolves will track a herd out in the fields. They'll target a weak one and try to slow just that one down. Meanwhile, their pack is catching up. They go attack and wound a young calf.

"It's just a couple wolves against an entire herd, so the entire herd might slow down, thinking they are protecting the calf. The next thing you know, they got a pack of wolves chewing on their asses. We ended up losing a couple cows instead of a calf.

"Listen, Sergeant... what I'm saying is, sure they could have called out, and then four, maybe five of them in the area could have run directly at our guns, but then what? Just a half dozen dead Primals."

"And?" Gyles asked, his frustration building. "What's the difference?"

"I think these things are pack hunters. Those two didn't cry out because they needed to go back and get their pack. These things are hunting us, Sergeant. Whether any of us likes it or not, they ain't as dumb as we want them to be."

Gyles gulped. He didn't want to swallow the prospect right now. "Let's just stay on mission; okay, Mega? Let's get this goofy bastard's truck and get these folks out of the church. We can worry about who is hunting who then."

"I heard that," Joe whispered. "And my truck is just yonder. And just like I tried to tell you, it's blocked in and surrounded by them damn things."

The men had stopped at a corner, where the alley met the main street. Gyles knew from the vantage of the tower that this street would lead back to the church if they traveled three blocks. But he also knew from the earlier viewpoint that the road was blocked. The alley emerged from the center of the block, and even with the screaming Primals behind them, for the moment, they were undetected.

Gyles moved to the corner of the building and peered around it. A half block away was a four-way intersection. Some sort of hasty roadblock had been erected and traffic was backed up in all directions with the Primals milling around between the stopped cars and barriers.

They were on the clogged side of the roadblock, destroyed bodies and mangled cars making crossing the street impossible for them. On the side of the street closest to them was a law office, and across the street, a convenience store with broken window fronts filled with the creatures. The street in between was clogged with loads of barriers.

In the northbound lane, was the eighteen-wheeler just as Joe had said, the nose facing the roadblock and the tail pointing out of town. The big rig was butted up against the stopped cars, but the back way appeared clear. Gyles pulled back in, away from the corner and paused, listening to the roar of the pursuing infected and the distant gunshots of the church battle.

He pressed his face close to Joe's. "Can you back it up?" he asked.

Joe snarled, "Of course I can back it up. Da hell kind of trucker do you think I am?"

The soldier shrugged. "Just trying to figure out why you ditched it in the first place."

"Because I wasn't going that way, asshole. The church is this way; why in the hell would I back up?" Joe said, his voice growing in volume.

Kenny pushed in. "Maybe to find a different route. One block over, I know for a fact that Michigan Avenue is open straight to the church. One road south, and you could have looped back to this alley."

Before Joe could respond, Gyles leaned back in. "You know this for a *fact*?"

"For a fact," Kenny said. "I came back through here on my own run to the Alamo a week or so ago. Police had some sort of roadblock, but they were just plastic barriers and sawhorses. All that shit was pushed aside and open. I drove my Honda Civic right through it."

"If he can get that truck started, can you guide us back to the church?" Gyles asked.

Kenny looked at the distant semi surrounded by the Primals. "Hell, yeah—too easy, Sergeant. It's east a few turns, and I can run that truck right down this same alley. But what about all of them things? You think those crazies will just let us walk in and drive off?"

"Let me worry about that detail. I just need you and this old coot to make sure the truck makes it back to the church," Gyles said.

Kenny leaned around the corner again. "Then, yeah, if we can get into the cab of that truck, I can get them to the church, no problem. Count on it."

Gyles pressed his back against the building behind him and turned to Mega. "How much ammo you got for the two-forty?"

Mega looked at his weapon then reached back and slapped his pack hanging low on his back. "Hundred in the gun, another two belts in my pack. Culver has my extra rounds."

Nodding, Gyles waved at Culver. "Hand it over."

Culver took a knee, removed his backpack, and pulled out a pair of 200-round belts of linked 7.62. He handed them across to Mega, who wrapped them over his shoulders Rambo style. "What you got planned, boss?" Culver whispered. "We about to make some trouble for these things?"

Shaking his head, Gyles looked back into the dark street behind them, listening to the pursuing growls as they grew louder. "Whatever is chasing us is getting closer. I need you to get these two into cover and hide there. I'm going to take Mega up on the roof of this law office and see if we can draw these things to us. We make enough noise, and you can get to the truck."

Culver hardened his jaw and shook his head no. "You'll be trapped. It's better if we all stick together."

Gyles grinned and leaned forward, looking around the corner again. "I don't think so; the road is clear ahead. You get that truck close to the buildings, and we can jump down to the roof, then we all get the hell out of here together."

Culver closed his eyes tight then slowly opened them. "Boss, this is one of those ideas that needs too many things to work, or it all goes to shit." He shook his head. "I don't like it. Let's just fight our way to the truck, go balls deep and fight our way out of here."

Nodding his acknowledgment but ignoring the recommendation, Gyles looked back at Mega, then pointed at a door in the building they were crouched next to. The sign over their head identified it as Curly and Sons, Attorneys at Law. "Get us inside," he whispered.

He turned back to Culver. "I'm not the mission, those kids at the church are. Remember that. Now, find a hiding spot within that traffic jam. You see an opportunity, break for that truck and get it running. Lock up tight and don't worry about us." Gyles listened for a second then looked at Kenny and continued. "You get the truck moving, clear out of those Primals, and run close to the buildings—we'll worry about getting on it." He stopped and looked at Joe. "Just don't take off too fast and leave us, you hear?"

"Loud and clear, soldier boy. I'll drive nice and slow next to the roof and give you a really soft landing pad."

Pointing a finger into the crowded street ahead, Gyles ordered, "Now go on, Culver—make yourself and these two disappear."

Culver looked back at him with disapproval on his face but bumped fists with Gyles, letting him know he understood. He turned ahead and crouched around the corner with Kenny and Joe close behind him. Gyles moved close to the edge, watching the trio make their way along the sidewalk then vanish into the mess of stalled vehicles.

Gyles squinted, staring into the mass of vehicles, trying to see where they went. He watched a yellow ambulance move slightly and a door close at its rear. He dipped his chin with approval; with them out of the way, the rest was up to him.

A hiss turned him back to Mega, who had a tomahawk out, ready to attack the office door. The man's eyes were fixed on the distant alley. Before Gyles could ask what he was waiting for, he looked in the direction the man was staring and saw the first of the pursuing Primals, a pair running ahead of an even larger pack. Gyles brought up his rifle. "Get us up to the roof. I got you covered," he said.

Soon, the *thwack!* of the tomahawk, the moan of the Primals, and the firing of his rifle filled the air.

CHAPTER FOURTEEN

DAY OF INFECTION, PLUS NINETEEN

East of Paris, Virginia

Luke squinted, looking into the darkness, unable to see the other end of the weapon. He froze then slowly raised his hand from the knob. He knew the others would pick up on his reactions and respond. If they hadn't already, a man would be taking position to fire rounds through the wall in the direction Luke was looking. They would kill anyone there before they allowed harm to come to him. He let his eyes shift and saw Weaver already aiming his rifle, taking slow steps to the left. Luke raised his arms higher and said, "Wait, it's okay!"

He took a short step back, catching Weaver's attention before the soldier lost his nerve and fired a salvo of green tip .223 rounds through the wall and into the man on the other side.

"It's okay, we aren't here to take anything," Luke

said, his voice calm and steady. He kept his hands in the air and continued to step away from the door. As he made distance on the door, he watched the shotgun barrel level and follow him onto the porch. Soon, an elderly, heavyset man in denim overalls moved behind it. The man had a thick white beard and a tight-fitting Farmall cap. "Da' hell ya'all doing out here?" he said.

The man's tired eyes searched the terrain behind Luke and stopped on the lined-up soldiers as he found them. The farmer could see that the soldiers had him out numbered and out gunned. Quickly, he took a short step back and raised a free hand, showing his palm while keeping the shotgun's barrel on Luke. "Now, I ain't asked for no trouble. You all's knocked on my door, not the other way around."

The man's head darted left and right, scanning the yard. He looked hard at the black-painted MRAP and then at Luke with his black tactical police vest, then again at the soldiers before stopping again on Luke. "What exactly is you all, anyhow? Soldiers or police?"

Luke smirked. "Bit of both, but I can tell you we mean you no harm. You can lower your weapon."

The man nudged his head toward the soldiers holding rifles at the low ready and said, "No harm, you say. That's not really how it's looking to me. I see a lot of men with guns in my front yard. I might seem simple to you all, but in these parts, that's not considered a friendly visit."

Looking back at Weaver, Luke put his arm out straight and waved his palm to the ground. The soldiers followed the command and let the rifles relax, dropping to the front, hanging on their slings, out of their hands but where they could be brought back into a fight in seconds. When his eyes moved back to the old man, his shotgun barrel was being slowly lowered and was soon hanging limp in his right arm. Luke nodded his appreciation at the action and extended his right hand. "I apologize for the way we came up on you. We were just expecting infected. Name's Luke. I was a deputy in a city west of here by the name of Vines."

"Vines, you say, huh?" The old man looked up toward the porch ceiling in deep thought, then returned the handshake. "I think I heard of Vines. My name's Earl. And you can relax—we ain't got any infected here. I heard plenty about them on the news but haven't seen one on this road, and certainly ain't had one on this farm."

"None?" Luke said. "Just ten miles from here, we've seen massive groups. The areas around the highway are swarming with them."

Earl nodded and grinned. "Yeah, I heard some-thing about that too." He squinted, then looked back at Luke as if an idea just popped into his head. "You know, as a matter of fact, there used to be some federal police that stopped by here every day. Guess they'd drive east down the road, check out some roadblock the state police had setup, then come on back. Feds said no infected bothered that roadblock, not a single one. They said it had something to do with the mountain; you know, the uphill and all. Apparently, the sick people—you know, the ones out walking around—well, they prefer to move downhill rather than up mountains. Guess they're lazy or something."

"I wouldn't put much faith in that," Weaver said, stepping closer. "I've seen them do some crazy things when they're chasing someone. Give them time, and they'll find this place."

Earl reached behind him and leaned his shotgun against the wall. "Funny enough, the Feds said something about that too. They said if I found a need to go down the mountain for anything, to make sure I'm not followed back. Seems the only way they figure on the infected getting this far is if they are chasing something." The man looked at the MRAP again. "Say, you all weren't followed, were you?"

Luke shook his head. "No, we broke contact with them far from here. Nothing followed us, but I really want you to understand, these things are unpredictable; they'll make their way up here soon enough. We just had a horde of them surround our camp. We had to fight our way out."

Earl rubbed at his thick beard and eyed Luke suspiciously. "What do you mean 'horde'? Horde of what?"

Before Luke could answer the question, a woman's voice called from in the house. Then she appeared in the doorway. She was as old as Earl but far shorter and thinner in stature. She looked at Luke, then the other soldiers, then turned to the old man and scowled. "Why haven't you invited these boys in? Have you completely lost your manners?"

Grinning, Earl put a hand on the woman's shoulder then stepped aside, holding open the door. "This here is my wife, Esther. She ain't much of a cook, but she does a decent job with breakfast, if you all would be interested," he said, waving them in.

"We wouldn't want to take your food, sir," Luke said before being pushed aside as the soldiers climbed the porch steps with Tucker leading the way.

"I would love a farm-cooked breakfast!" Weaver said, following the others in, leaving Luke standing alone on the porch.

Earl shrugged and winked at Luke then pointed to the girl left alone on the lawn. "Well, you two may as well join them. And don't worry about our supplies— we have plenty. This is a real working farm, and our stores are stocked."

Luke nodded and waved for Kate to enter the farm-house then followed Earl inside. The man turned and closed the door, but Luke noticed he didn't lock it. They'd entered a large family room that butted up against a formal dining room. At the back of the wide room with tall ceilings was a long table made of dark wood, where the soldiers had already made themselves comfortable. Luke could hear them hooting and making jokes as they passed dishes.

"Sorry about them, they don't get out much," Luke said, pointing to the group of men digging through a large basket of bread as Esther filled glasses with milk.

Laughing, Earl said, "Don't you worry none about them. Esther is used to feeding the farm hands. Matter of fact, she probably misses the action." The man rubbed his belly. "I try, but even I can't eat enough to keep that woman busy."

Luke looked toward the back of the room. "Farm hands? You have more people here?"

Shaking his head, the old man said, "No, not recently." He put a hand on Luke's back and guided him into the dining room as he spoke. "I had a half dozen men but cut them loose when this started. The radio said people should lock up and stay indoors, so I sent them all home to their people.

"The man on the TV said something about we should wait and stay indoors until told otherwise."

Earl paused a beat and indicated an empty chair, where Luke sat. Then Earl pulled out a chair near the head of the table and sat next to him. The man filled a cup from a coffee pot then placed it back on the table. "The newsman made it sound like it would only be a few days, but as you can see, here we are, still waiting."

Studying the coffee pot, Luke waited for the go-ahead from Earl then filled his own cup. "These federal police you said stopped by the farm, who are they?" Luke said.

The old man took a sip from the cup and raised an eyebrow. "You serious? The folks at the complex up there... some sort of security, I guess. The Weather Station or whatever it is they're calling it these days."

"Mount Weather?" Luke asked.

Earl laughed again. "Yeah, I've heard it called that a time or two. Never been up that way myself, but some of my hands have done work up there for extra money, construction or whatnot." He sipped the coffee again, holding back his hands as Esther approached and scooped a helping of hash onto his plate.

He looked back at Luke. "Anyhow, day or so after this all started... convoys of trucks moved up the mountain, headed that way. Army trucks, school busses, all of it. Later, we'd heard about all the troubles in Washington on the TV."

He paused as Esther filled Luke's plate then continued. "But still, the only folks we saw was all the traffic up the Mountain. Not many of them bothered stopping; most were in an awful hurry. Like I said, the radio and TV were giving people instructions to stay put. But we were hearing things from people on the road, official-type people saying it was wise to pack up and head for the hills." He laughed again. "Fools. We already are in the hills."

Luke grinned at the remark then, using a fork, took in a heap of the potatoes, peppers, onions, and corned beef mixture. It was delicious. He looked at Earl with wide eyes. "Damn Earl, if this is just decent, then you have a sophisticated palate, my friend."

The old man smiled. "You get as much of it as you want, or I'll be eating it for days."

Luke took another bite then looked back to the front door. "You said there were other travelers on the road?"

Earl dipped his chin. "Yeah, official types, mostly. Not sure who they were, but the traffic didn't last long.

The Feds said there were roadblocks or something the military put up. The government wanted people locked down to prevent the spread of infection. I assume it worked; ain't seen no infected up this way but haven't really heard. The radio and TV just shut off one day, and shortly after that, the Fed boys stopped coming by."

Earl scratched at the side of his head. "Come to think of it, you might be the first to have stopped here in over a week. Was sort of hoping you might have some news on what's happening down the mountain."

Luke sighed and took another sip of the coffee. "Well, as I was saying earlier, there are hordes just down the mountain."

Earl nodded. "You saying hordes; you mean, like herds? Like herds of what? People and such?"

Luke's face turned hard. "These infected, they're something else, Earl. If you haven't seen one, it's hard to explain exactly what it is." Luke looked into his coffee cup before sipping. He sighed and looked back at Earl. "Think of a person becoming a rabid wolf. That's what they are like, crazy violent. They can't be reasoned with... all they want to do is kill. Then imagine a pack of those wolves, then a hundred packs of them." Luke paused, he could see that the men around the table had stopped eating and were looking at him. "That, my friend, is what a horde is."

"You're serious, ain't ya?" Earl asked, the old man's forehead changing from red to a pale white. "So... it's all true, what the news was saying about the attacks in the cities."

"I'm afraid so," Luke said. "I don't know how you've managed to avoid them, but they will find this place. And the things about them not coming up the mountain..." He shook his head. "That might work for a while, but they came after my group, and we were deep in the national forest. We were far off the county road, and they still found us."

"And the military roadblocks, at least they're working to hold them all back?" Earl asked.

Luke shook his head again. "Roadblocks, no. Dead, all of them, all dead." He sighed. "The only military still operating that I know is at a camp just east of here, and when we left, they were in a lot of trouble. And that roadblock your federal buddies were manning down the mountain, I found it abandoned."

Earl looked at the faces of the men around the table. "So, what about you all? You deserters then? Why ain't you back at your base with the others?"

Weaver stood, his mood suddenly shifting. "No, sir, we aren't deserters. We were sent here. We have a mission at Mount Weather, and all of us are hoping there is something up there that can help us with all of this."

"And what exactly might that be?"

The soldier shook his head. "Not certain, but if the government is still operating up there, we need to find out." He faced his men. "Wrap it up, boys. These folks have been mighty hospitable, but the sun is breaking the horizon, and we need to get back on the road," he said before turning to leave the room.

Luke pushed back from his chair and looked at Earl. "Sir, we really do appreciate the meal and the information. If there is something we could do for you in exchange, just ask. Maybe escort you all up to the mountain, to the base?"

Earl laughed. "No, son. We're just fine right here. Like we said, we ain't seen any of those infected. I'm sure it will all clear up soon enough, and things can get back to normal."

Standing, Luke could see that the other men were leaving the dining room, with Kate close behind. Esther was already scrambling to collect dishes. He turned back to the old man. "I really wish you would reconsider. When those things make their way up here, it'll be like nothing you've ever seen before."

The old man smiled softly and rubbed his beard. "I think we'll be just fine. But I tell ya what—first sign of trouble, and I'll put the woman in my old Ford truck and head up that way." He reached out and slapped Luke's shoulder. "Now go on, it looks like your friends are in a hurry."

CHAPTER FIFTEEN

DAY OF INFECTION, PLUS NINETEEN

North of Hayslette, Virginia

Gyles adjusted his point of aim; with two quick trigger pulls, muzzle flashes lit the alley like lightning strikes. He heard screaming then saw a body fall, and he fired again, faster this time. Blinking his eyes rapidly, he tried to focus through the rifle smoke and strobing lights. He heard himself yelling, taunting the crazies as he fell into his own personal killing zone. But this wasn't a blocking action—he couldn't get too deeply engaged or he would be lost here. No, he needed to shoot and move. His brain was stalling when it needed to speed up.

He cursed himself, feeling the combat's trance fall over him like a warm blanket. He knew exactly what it was but still couldn't fight it. It was a mental state that had killed men better than him. A place you parked your senses, firing, working your weapon like a finely tuned instrument, the battle a concert, and he was leading an M4 carbine solo.

Forgetting to take cover, forgetting to fall back or move ahead, not changing positions, suddenly the enemy fixed on you, and you were dead. His mind continued to bounce... shifting aim, killing the enemy, reloading. He was comfortable here, but he knew he needed to focus on the fight ahead.

"Sergeant, what the fuck are you doing?" he heard Mega scream.

He was back. He stood and fired off another volley, this time hitting a large man twice in the center of the chest. It was not enough to kill it, but the second shot destroyed the Primal's spinal column, sending it crashing to the street. No time to see what he'd done, the soldier was already searching for another target, finding a sprinter closing in on them from the left.

He shifted his point of aim and fired, working the trigger rapidly, feeling the buffer spring work with every shot, watching brass cartwheel from the ejection port. This time the third shot clipped the top of the Primal's head. He spun back to see Mega fumbling with the hawk and the door's lock.

"Just kick in the damn door! We need to get off this street now!" he shouted.

Mega looked back. His face was pale, his eyes wide with fear. He had the shank of his hawk pressed into the doorframe, prying with all his weight. The wood protested with creaks and moans but wouldn't give. He turned to Gyles. "Sergeant, if I break the door down, we won't be able to close it behind us. Those things will just follow us in."

"Mega, I swear to everything holy, kick in the damn door, or we are going to die on this street!"

Gyles snapped back to the front and fired the last rounds in his magazine then pressed the release, letting the box magazine clang on the street. He reached for his hip and pulled a frag grenade. After yanking the pin, he tossed it as far down the alley as he could before snatching a reload from his chest and slapping the magazine home. He was back up, firing again before the grenade exploded somewhere to his front. A dumpster exploded, bursting into flames and dumping its contents across the alley. Not bothering to take cover, he heard the buzz of frag zipping over his head. He pushed left against Mega, completely out of patience. "Kick in the damn door, or get out of the way."

Mega backed off, roared, and ran at the building. The door seemed to explode under the big man's weight, bursting inward. Gyles backstepped into the entrance, still firing into the now smoke-filled alley before throwing a second frag grenade into the void. He looked behind him to find Mega sprawled out on the floor. He reached down and pulled the man to his feet, and with his face inches from the soldier, he ordered, "Stairs! Find the stairs now!"

Mega's eyes swiveled in his head. He'd obviously taken a hard blow from the collision with the door. He wavered then pointed at a sign at the end of the room. At one time, it was probably illuminated, but even in the low light, both men could read the stairs symbol. "Go, go, go!" Gyles shouted.

He peeled off the doorway and shoved the big soldier toward the sign. Gyles rushed back to the entry and kicked a receptionist desk over, blocking the doorway, then threw a filing cabinet on top for good measure. The dumpster fire was now lighting the alley. He could hear the closing Primals screaming outside. He looked back and watched Mega stagger toward the stairwell door.

"Please don't be locked, please don't be locked," Gyles shouted as he ran for the end of the room. He knew they wouldn't have time to breach a second door; they would get through, or the fight would end here.

A crash behind him let him know that the Primals had reached the hasty entrance barricade. Ahead, Mega had the steel fire door open and was standing in front of it, like he was holding the door for an old lady. Gyles came at him like a defensive tackle, hitting the big guy hard with his shoulder, launching him into the tight corridor. Gyles scrambled back to his feet and dove for the fire door. He gripped the pull bar and yanked the door toward him, quickly finding out how fortunate they were that the door opened out. Just as the first of the Primals found it, they crashed into it, shoving the door tightly closed. Gyles felt the shudder in the building as more of the things crammed against the opening.

A soft green glow suddenly filled the space. He turned to see Mega had snapped out of his daze and had tossed a chem light into the corner. Gyles rested his eyes on it then yanked a fire extinguisher off the wall that was mounted just above it. He pulled his fighting knife and cut the black rubber hose from the extinguisher then forced the length of hose through the door's locking mechanism, extending a bolt latch into a locked position.

It was sloppy, but even without the loose tie job, he could feel the weight of the Primals pressing against the door. He pushed lightly and felt the force of them keeping the door in the closed position. "Come on, Mega, we have some time before they figure out how to get this open, we need to get to the roof."

Mega grimaced. The big man's nose was bleeding, his pupils dilated like saucers in the green light. Gyles looked at him. "You okay, buddy?"

"Just got my bell rung, is all. I'm still in the fight, Sergeant," Mega mumbled.

Gyles nodded. "I know you are—take a minute to collect your shit. We're moving up top in one."

He took note of Mega's clumsy attempts at going over his kit and knew he was struggling, but he needed the soldier to stay at high tempo. Now wasn't a time to play mother hen and allow the man to drop his guard. Gyles watched his friend take a drink from a canteen and strap his tomahawk back to his thigh. The big soldier was a warfighter who knew what was at stake. If Mega was lagging, it was because he was hurting, but Gyles knew the man would do everything to push the hurt aside and Charlie Mike (continue mission).

Gyles turned toward the glowing light and checked his own chest rig, finding three empty magazine pouches. It was bad form to have dropped the empty mags in the street, but dying during a reload was also bad form. He had boxes of ammunition in his pack, but no spare magazines beyond what he carried in his rig. He sorted himself out, replacing the chest pouches with fresh mags from his hips... better to have them close than having to reach. He then replaced the expended frag grenades with two others from his pack. It would have to do for now. He turned to the corner, picked up the chem light, and tossed it up the stairwell to the next landing.

Turning to Mega, he said, "You ready, big hoss?"

"I got this, Sergeant... easy day, easy day," Mega grunted, using the handrail to pull himself to his feet.

"Easy day." Gyles forced a grin and nodded. "I'll take point. Be ready to fill in if I need it."

Stepping off and following the left wall with his shoulder, Gyles pointed the way with his rifle's barrel. He reached the next landing and stepped over the chem light, leaving it where it had fallen. He felt a damp breeze on his face and looked up. The roof exit door was slightly ajar, allowing in glimmers of low light. He stood for a moment, listening and waiting, only smelling the smoke of fires, and not the death and decay of Primals.

He pulled the rifle tighter into the pocket of his shoulder and planted his feet. Gyles looked down at Mega and pointed at the door then put a finger to his lips. The big man nodded his reply and Gyles moved out, sidestepping, slicing angles toward the doorway. At the top of the stairs was a double landing, a large L-shaped space with the door at the end of the short leg. Scanning left and right, he could see the landing was empty, the floor clear. He searched the walls and floor but saw no signs of forced entry or battle damage.

Gyles shuffle-stepped to the entrance with his rifle up then eased the door the rest of the way open. Outside, he found the rooftop visible in the orange light of early dawn. He tried to listen for dangers, but it was impossible with the screaming of the infected below him and surrounding the building outside. His eyes searched, and he saw a survivors' camp—or what was once a form of one. At one time, people had moved furniture and curtains up here. Bed rolls and clothing lay piled in corners. A barebeque grill was in the middle, near an air conditioning unit. Ropes, tied to antennas, still had fabric draped over them. A large, red-painted S.O.S. had been hand scrawled across a white curtain that wafted in the breeze like a flag. Gyles moved another half dozen steps then waited for Mega to close in behind him.

"You see anyone?" Mega said in a loud whisper.

Gyles shook his head no. They were alone; the hastily constructed survivors' camp was empty—no bodies, no luggage, not even any trash. Whoever had once holed up here had abandoned it days ago or been evacuated. Together, they rotated in a 360, searching and scanning the remaining spaces to ensure they were alone on the rooftop.

With a look at Mega, Gyles pointed to the door. "Lock it up the best you can," he whispered. He covered the shadows as Mega pushed the door shut and pressed a board below the handle, jamming it closed.

"'Bout all we can do without tools," the big man said with a shrug.

There wasn't much more that could be done to hold it, but, working quickly, Gyles and Mega piled up what was left of the camp in front of and around the door. Then Gyles moved to the edge of the roof. The perimeter was covered with a short knee wall, no more than two feet tall. In the street below, he could see the Primals had closed in, looking up at him with their eyes reflecting the new sun. The two men were effectively surrounded on the rooftop. His stomach began to twist, and he wanted to vomit at the prospects of what he had done, allowing himself to be cornered.

He shook his head and closed his eyes, took a deep breath and opened them again. They weren't cornered yet. It was all part of the plan, and the plan was working, he assured himself. He walked back toward the intersection side of the law office. Scanning, he found the ambulance his men were hidden in. To the far right of it, less than one hundred feet away, was the semi-truck with a large box trailer attached to it. He looked up and down the length of the trailer. Only a few of the Primals were still near it, but they were all moving in his direction.

The sound of glass breaking pulled his attention to the ground floor below. A large, street-facing window had collapsed from pressure of the Primals against it. The creatures were now pouring inside. He wasn't too concerned, knowing that it helped him. The more of the things packed into the room, the less likely they would be able to get the bottom stairwell door open. The more the merrier.

It was time to work. He needed to clear a path for his men on the ground. Looking back at Mega, Gyles said, "Get your gun up and start greasing as many of these things as possible."

Mega looked down at the swirling mob, then back at him. "Seriously? I can just start killing them?" the man said almost eagerly.

Gyles swallowed hard then dipped his chin. "Yeah, light them up. But short bursts—you need to stretch out the ammo as long as you can. Shoot at the ones further away to draw them in. The ones inside and around the building are right where we want them."

The man's smile vanished, and his eyebrows tightened. "You don't want me to kill the ones trying to get up at us? You want even more of them down there?"

Gyles shook his head. "No, don't kill the ones in tight. I want them there; we need to get our boys out of that ambulance and into that truck. Once that's done, we'll start worrying about our exit plan." Gyles thought for a beat, then continued, "Mega, you need to make damn sure you save us some ammo to get away. You got that?"

"Got it, boss. Kill a bunch but save some killing for later," Mega said, dropping his pack and extending the bi-pod on his machine gun. Soon the man was posted up on the knee wall, a belt of ammo laid out flat, ready to let rounds fly.

Steps away, Gyles found a location where he had a clear lane of fire over the ambulance and the soldiers' path to the truck. If anything popped up, he would have to kill it; the men on the ground couldn't risk a shot and attracting any attention. If they fired and were drawn into a fight down in the open, it was over. He also had the responsibility to cover the machine gunner's blind spots and the rooftop door, in case the infected managed to break through. He had started to reconsider the setup, maybe moving the M240 to the opposite corner, when Mega let loose with his first burst of gunfire.

The man whooped. "Get some!" he shouted as he let go with several shorter bursts.

Gyles looked at the traffic jam and could see Primal heads popping up. Ones that had avoided the fight before were now running toward the law office. More emerged from down the street, hearing the gunfire. From all directions, they were on the way, running at the man on the roof who was shouting into the crazed mob of infected. Gyles didn't know if it was the noise of the machine gun, the yellow flames launching from the barrel, or the obscene man screaming at them, but every eye seemed to turn, every infected in the neighborhood now in a full-on frenzy.

Gyles looked at the ambulance and saw it still sitting motionless. He panned toward the truck and could see a trio of the infected standing near the cab of the semi. Unlike the others that were running directly at them, the trio at the truck appeared to be observing the massacre without emotion. Gyles shook his head, reconsidering his previous thoughts. He snarled and spit off the roof. "Well, if you don't want to come to the party, then I'll bring the party to you," he said and raised his weapon, putting his eye to his rifle's optic.

The three were odd, almost human-like, and not as wounded as others he had seen. But the trio didn't belong together. A woman with short-cropped hair, wearing a torn pantsuit, looked like she should be closing on a million-dollar real estate deal. Next to her was a tall man in denim skinny jeans and a black hipster jacket. The last was a thick-chested, tan-skinned man in a bloodstained white tank top, his arms covered in bad tattoos. They were obviously infected but acting more like the pair he'd spotted earlier in the alley.

Smart ones, he thought to himself. *But not that smart.*

He assumed the presence of the trio was the reason his men were still hiding in the ambulance. They had their route blocked to get to the truck. Gyles centered the cross hairs on the largest of the three and fired. He watched a black spot appear on the big man's white tank top. The creature hardly staggered. It didn't look down, it didn't flinch; instead, its eyes remained locked on the chaos at the building. Gyles adjusted his point of aim and pulled the trigger again. This time, the left side of the man's face zipped away. The creature stammered then fell forward onto the pavement. The woman in the pantsuit looked down at the body for a moment, then her eyes locked on Gyles.

"Shit," he whispered, a chill traveling up his spine. "How does she know it was me?"

Instead of carrying on the mental debate, he shifted his point of aim again and fired on the now screaming woman. The round went low, hitting her in the right shoulder, spinning her counterclockwise. Gyles looked for the hipster, but he wasn't there. He went back to the woman, who'd regained her balance and was now running with a dangling right arm. He led the target and fired three times. The last two shots sent the creature tumbling under a minivan, making him unable to see if it was dead.

"That'll have to do," he whispered then continued to scan the traffic for the hipster, but he was gone.

Back to the ambulance, he could see that the rear door was now open, and his men were moving out in single file. Kenny was in the front, ahead of Joe, and Culver took up the slack position. Gyles ignored the damage Mega was doing so he could provide overwatch for his team on the ground. The path was clear. They moved quickly, and soon Joe was in the cab of the truck. He observed as Kenny and Culver piled in through a door on the other side.

He couldn't hear the big vehicle's engine start over the machine gun and the roar of the infected, but he saw the black smoke belch from the exhaust pipes. The big diesel engine revved just as Mega was changing belts in the machine gun. Dropping into reverse, the truck screeched, then a loud beeping sound filled the air when the truck began to move. The Primals surrounding the building all at once fell silent. Slowly, their attention turned to the truck in the congested street. Gyles saw Hipster Primal emerge from the cars. It leaped onto the roof of a silver Lexus, pointed at the big rig, and arched its back, howling.

"There you are," Gyles said. He lined up his optic, fired, and watched rounds tear into the hipster.

The infected around the building changed direction, now focused on the truck. "Cut them down!" Gyles ordered, pointing at the shifting mass.

Mega swiveled his position and fired into the waves of infected charging at the semi, their bodies ripping apart as they reached the street filled with cars. Rounds skipped off the pavement and tore through the infected, punching holes into vehicles. Slowly, the truck backed farther and farther away. Gyles concentrated his own fire on any of the Primals chasing it in the street. Soon the truck was beyond the intersection. It stopped and then moved forward, turning right down a block, driving away from them.

"Cease fire!" Gyles yelled, ducking below the wall

and out of sight of the infected on the ground. Mega turned back and saw him. Quickly, he did the same, pulling the weapon off the wall and dropping to his back. He rolled over and crawled to Gyles. "What are we doing? Kind of late to hide, they already know we're up here," Mega whispered.

"We need to get out of here. Once Kenny gets clear of that mob, he will be looping back for us. We need to be ready when they get here."

CHAPTER SIXTEEN

DAY OF INFECTION, PLUS NINETEEN

Blue Ridge Mountain Road, Virginia

L uke rested his hands on the top of the steering wheel and surveyed the terrain around him. The trees had suddenly opened and created a wide grassy area on both sides. Debris and brush had all been cut back to the sides of the road, revealing a chain link fence that ran as far as they could see.

For the last five miles, he'd observed nothing but forest and the occasional gated driveway disappearing into the dark trees that lined the road. Even when they had seen a home on the mountain pass, it appeared to be abandoned, the same as the farm looked from the outside. No signs of people, animals, or any other activity. He looked at Weaver, who was studying the hand-drawn map.

"You know, I was expecting something more ominous... broken down cars, burnt houses," Luke said.

"It's like this entire place has been spared from all of it. They are either all gone or hiding."

Weaver shook his head. "No, not spared—there's just no traffic, no people, because they have been moved. Anyone that was here must have been evacuated, probably by force. I think we are on the cusp of a no-man's land."

"No-man's land? What? Like a buffer zone?" Luke asked.

Shrugging, Weaver said, "Maybe not intentional, but like a fire break."

"Fire break?" Luke asked.

The soldier nodded. "Like a forest fire. You know, how they work out ahead and cut those wide lanes in the forest so when the fire hits it, it just sort of burns out. The fire has no place to go, and it's already used up all of its fuel, so it just stops." He thought again. "The old man said the federal police warned them to not let the infected follow them up the mountain. Well, remove all the people and there is nothing left to follow."

"So you think someone got smart enough in all the chaos, worked ahead, and removed all the people out of this area so the virus couldn't spread. Like it would just die off and stop here. Not move up this valley."

Weaver rubbed his chin, his face showing that he was reconsidering his original theory. He looked back at the map and traced his finger over the contour lines of the mountain. "No, not that exactly. But someone could have just cut out a vacuum to slow infected in just this one area. You know, like they were protecting something. We figured it out in all of five minutes. I'm sure people smarter than us wouldn't have struggled with the concept."

"Mount Weather then?" Luke asked. "You think they did this to protect the facility?"

Weaver put the map back on the console and pointed straight ahead. "I guess we'll find out soon enough. According to Gus's map, we should see a cutoff to the installation up here in these woods."

"Yeah, well, I don't want to wait that long," Luke said. He killed the engine on the truck and parked in the center of the road they were traveling north on.

"What are you doing?" Weaver asked.

Luke undid the latch on the driver's door and swung it open. Lifting his rifle, he stepped out onto the street. "Stay with the truck. I just want to scout ahead a bit and see what's up there," he said without looking back.

He moved forward, but before he reached the front side, Weaver was out, standing beside him. Luke frowned then continued his trek toward the chain link fencing. He stepped just off the road and into the long grass. He ran a hand over the tops of the blades of grass. "This has been cut recently, within the last couple weeks."

"After the infection then," Weaver said.

"Or just after." Luke nodded and looked at the fence, studying a small sign.

Every twenty feet along the fence, a placard hung.

US GOVERNMENT, NO TRESPASSING. The fence itself was ten feet high with Y posts at the top, supporting triple strands of barbed wire. Just enough to keep an honest person out.

Weaver shrugged. "This isn't anything out of the ordinary, bro. All bases have fences and signs like this."

Luke nodded and continued to carefully study the fence line. Looking a bit farther down the road, he could see that the fence on the eastern side had been screened off with black fabric to prevent anyone from looking in. He scanned his eyes along the base of the fence and could just make out a hidden gate.

"That screen," Luke said in a low voice. "That's to hide whatever they got inside. Is that normal too?"

"I mean, it's not abnormal. It's not completely weird or anything." Weaver watched Luke study the terrain. "What are you looking for, anyway? The main gate is probably up the road."

Luke put his hands on his hips and spun around again, looking in all directions, then pointed at the screened-in security barriers. "The fence is on both sides of the road, and we seem to be traveling down the center of the reservation. I imagine, like you mentioned, a main facility gate is up ahead."

He walked back to the shoulder and knelt by the screened fence again, picking up a handful of rocks and letting them fall back to the ground as he rolled them through his fingers. "Look at the color of these rocks right here in this section," he said, "Doesn't match the others on the shoulder of the road."

"Yeah, so what, Tonto? You're wasting time. Let's head for the main gate," Weaver said.

Luke shook his head. "No. I don't think that's the best play. I guess we have a decision to make."

Weaver walked closer and slung his rifle over his shoulder. "A decision? I thought we already decided."

"Yeah, we know what we're here to do, but how do we expect to do it?" Luke said softly, keeping his eyes on the black-fabric-covered fencing on the right side of the road.

"Well, we came to shut down the tower," Weaver said. "We have plenty of bang in that bag, so let's go find it and blow the hell out of it."

Luke dropped the rest of the gravel and walked farther down the road, approaching the concealed screened gate. Weaver snorted as if he'd just seen it there. The gate was constructed to look like part of the fence. Double-sided and large enough to fit wide vehicles through it, the gate had the same fabric stretched across the opening. Luke ran his hand along the poles, searching for a locking mechanism. He found two large push bars that ran through rings and into a mechanism on the far side, where they couldn't be reached by anyone on the road.

He grabbed the fence and pulled, testing its sturdiness. Then he leaped up, grabbing the links and pulling himself up just high enough to see over the fabric. He hung there for a moment before dropping back to the ground.

"Just what I was expecting," Luke said, stepping

back. "That gravel over there is also new, and so is this gate. The metal on these sections isn't worn down and tarnished like the rest of the fence. It was recently cut, and this dropped in."

"You want to tell me what exactly this is supposed to mean?" Weaver asked.

"This was just added probably around the time the grass was cut. Someone chopped a hole and added a gate here to let vehicles rapidly pass in and out. On the other side, there is a field full of shipping containers. If I had to give you a reasonable guess, I'd say they cordoned off the larger facility and staged something here." Luke smiled at Weaver and began walking back to the MRAP. Over his shoulder he said, "But more importantly, I don't see any security on the other side. No towers, no cameras, nothing. This was hasty and single purpose—to get loads of materials in. Then they shut it all down and walked away from it."

At the side of the MRAP, Luke opened a compartment above the tires and removed a large pair of bolt cutters and began walking back toward the gate.

"What? We just going to bust in over here?" Weaver said. "We do that, and there are guards on the inside, they won't be happy."

Luke laughed. "I've been thinking about that. If there are guards inside, what do you think they will have to say when you tell them we're here to blow up their tower?"

Laughing ,Weaver shook his head and looked hard

at Luke. "You think sneaking in and blowing it up will go over any better?"

"We are about to find out," Luke said, this time with a genuine smile.

He moved to the gate and set the teeth of the bolt cutters on the lower section of lock bar. He pushed the handles together, and the bar snapped with little resistance. He moved to the top of the second bar and repeated the action. The lock bars fell away, and the gate pressed in, now only held by the black fabric. Luke passed the bolt cutters back to Weaver. He pulled out his KA-BAR knife and cut a long slit in the fabric. With the screening gone, the gates easily swung in, exposing a rough dirt road on the other side.

Just as Luke had seen before, the road ran through a field, both sides of it stacked deep with shipping containers. Beyond the rows, they could see the long fingers of a communications antenna. "Stay here while I move the truck off the road."

Weaver moved back to the gate and pulled both sides wider and watched as Luke drove the black MRAP through and parked it tight between two high stacks of shipping containers. It stuck out like a sore thumb, but it was better than leaving it on the road. The vehicle's ramp dropped, and soldiers poured out as Weaver worked to re-secure the gate and pull the fabric back over it. Then he grabbed his own gear from the vehicle.

Luke moved onto the dirt road, wearing a light backpack and carrying his rifle. Kate, the young girl, was by his side. "Let's take us a walk. I have a feeling the place is abandoned, or at least all moved underground."

"What if it's not?" Kate asked.

Luke stopped and looked at her then at the others. "If we are confronted, we surrender. Remember, we are just survivors from Camp Alamo, looking for help. Nothing more."

"Are we taking the demo charges?" Tucker asked.

Luke grimaced and shook his head. "What demo charges?" he said sarcastically. "I just said, we're from Camp Alamo, looking for help."

Weaver returned from the truck with his pack on and his rifle slung. "We got it, deputy, now just lead the way."

Looking around a last time, and confident they were alone, Luke stepped off with the girl still beside him. Weaver hung back on the road, and the rest of the men staggered their positions. The container field stretched on for the length of two football fields, then the dirt road connected with a paved one that continued off to the northeast. Ahead, on the right, was an empty parking lot and a large, square, steel-sided building with no windows.

Luke kept them walking the road, the team examining the building as they passed. He felt Weaver close in beside him. "Building looks intact and closed up," Weaver whispered. "Maybe we should take a look."

"Not what we're here for, is it?" Luke said. He

looked at the empty parking lot Weaver was staring at. "They probably sent all the civilians home."

"Or sent them into the doomsday bunker to ride this thing out," Weaver replied.

Shaking his head no, Luke said, "Nope, no cars, and I doubt they would waste space on some civilian staffers. Typical non-essential workers probably went home to their families. Like I said before, I expect to find this place closed from outer appearances, all locked up tighter than bark on a tree."

Weaver turned in a circle while keeping his pace beside Luke. He pointed with his jaw to the east, where a large tower reached into the sky. "It looks big enough, you think that's our target?"

"I do," Luke said without slowing his pace.

They continued past the steel building then approached another empty lot that paralleled a smaller office building. Farther down the road, they spotted another complex with several structures, but that didn't take their interest as much as a fenced-in field off to the east. Inside the fenced perimeter was not only the base of the tall radio tower, but also several concrete platforms, housing large satellite dishes and radio antennas that orbited the massive tower.

"That's what we're looking for," Luke said. He stopped and put his hands on his hips then turned slowly, taking in the geography around him.

Tucker grunted from behind him. "We don't have enough bang for all of that."

Luke nodded in agreement. "We need to be smart,

fellas. There has got to be a central control for all of this stuff, power, communications, we take that down and this will go with it."

"Hell, that could be hundreds of feet below ground," Weaver exclaimed.

Luke pointed to a small steel building with *High Voltage* signs painted on the sides. "Or it could be right in front of us."

They walked along the fence, finding a gate. This time, it was made of heavy steel and designed to slide in and out on heavy rollers. The top of the fence was lined with coiled razor wire. There would be no cutting or climbing in. Luke walked along the sliding gate and found a keypad with a magnetic card reader. Without bothering to touch the pad, he turned and pointed to a small building nearest them connected to the gate by a sidewalk. "Let's check it out."

The building was short and narrow. From a distance, it had the appearance of an oversized garage. But on closer inspection, they could see that there were dark tinted windows in the sides and a small parking lot with four vacant spots beside it. Two of the spots were filled with white pickup trucks, the sides filled with toolboxes. Luke moved past the vehicles and found another keypad and card reader at the building's entrance. He shook his head and continued on, following the building around. He tapped at the dark tinted windows. "Ballistic glass," he said.

"We could shoot our way in," Tucker said.

"I just said it's ballistic glass—as in bullet and blast proof," Luke grunted.

He kept walking until he saw a large central air conditioning unit. He turned his head sideways then looked back at the others. "It's running." He moved closer and put his hand on the unit, feeling the subtle vibrations. As if someone was looking to confirm his assessment, the unit kicked on and a large fan began to turn.

Luke stepped away from the unit and followed the wall to a dumpster. He climbed on top of it then jumped up, grabbing the edge of the roof, and pulled himself to the top. Looking along the roof, he saw a small utility hatch secured by a standard padlock. He looked down at the team on the ground and grinned. "Meet me at the front door."

Moving to the hatch, he took a knee and examined the hasp. The screws holding it were loosed and stripped. He used his KA-BAR to get under the flat edge then popped the hasp from the aluminum door. The hatch flipped open easily on well-worn hinges. Looking down, he could just make out the shape of a narrow utility room in the soft glow of emergency lighting. He swung his legs in first, his boots hitting the rungs of a narrow roof access ladder. He dropped to the floor and saw the room was lined with full shelves of cleaning supplies. Walking the space, he found an open a door at the end that exited into a long hallway.

Luke stepped out onto a high-gloss polished floor. He paused as the cold air from the air conditioner hit his face then he closed his eyes, listening to the low hum of the building's mechanics. There was nothing else, no clack of closing doors, no cross talk from a water cooler conversation, no footfalls in the hallway. He turned and looked both directions again, seeing nothing but hallway and glossy floor tile. Certain he was alone, he turned and moved left toward where he thought the entrance should be.

He spotted the main entrance door near the corner of the building, but he hesitated when he saw a small closed-circuit camera monitor mounted high on the wall. The grainy video showed his team waiting just outside on the walkway. He grimaced, suddenly concerned with who else may be monitoring these cameras. It was too late to worry about that now; they were committed.

To the left of the door was a green button mounted to a black plate. Stenciled in red above it was a warning placard: AUTHORIZED PERSONNEL ONLY. As if the placard wasn't enough, someone had pinned a memo to the wall. Luke attempted to read it in the low light of the hallway. There were a lot of *by order of this* and *under the authority of that,* and several threats, but the summary was, "Don't let anyone in the door if they do not have a badge or authorized escort."

Luke grinned before he reached up and snatched the memo off the wall. He wadded it and tossed it down the hallway then pressed the button with a stiff middle finger. There was a buzz and a click. Soon after, the outer door opened, letting in the blinding sunlight. He squinted and watched his team enter the building then close the doors behind them, all of them now basking in the cool air.

With his team inside, he moved into a small alcove on the far side of the door that he hadn't noticed before. Nothing close to a lobby, it was just enough space for a pair of chairs and coat racks. On the back wall behind the chairs were wooden cubbyholes. He randomly scanned a few of them, finding nothing. To the right of the cubbies was another instruction placard informing the building's visitors to power off all electronic devices and to leave them there while in the building. Luke pointed at the sign.

"Any of you all got cell phones?" he said sarcastically.

All the men laughed except Tucker, who pulled a phone from his pocket. "I ain't leaving my phone, got pictures of my girls on here," he said adamantly.

"Girls, as in plural?" Luke asked.

Tucker began to answer, but before he could, Luke raised his hand. "No, no, never mind. I really don't want to know." This caused more laughter from the group. "Just put that shit back in your pocket, Tucker." He shook his head again at the sign and dropped his pack.

"Let's unload our gear here while we clear the building," he said.

The others followed his action, and soon they were all out of their heavy packs, except Kate, who refused to let go of her tiny backpack. Luke looked at her and nodded, then said, "Let's break into two teams and clear the building. Tucker, you and Kate are with me. Sergeant Weaver, you have the rest of the guys." He turned and pointed down the hall "Listen, if a door is locked, then leave it like you found it. I don't want to break anything and trigger any alarms. People or no people, we don't need the noise. Let's take a simple stroll, look for anything out of place, and meet back here to plan."

The men replied with nods, unslinging rifles and taking them at the low ready. Enough light was already coming in the windows that they didn't need lights or night vision goggles. Luke watched Weaver pull his group aside and go over his and their equipment. Watching them work, Luke finally realized he had somehow taken command of this small team. He cursed himself; leadership over the group was the last thing he wanted. This was something he'd been running away from since he'd left the Marine Corps, but still, it always managed to come back and bite him in the ass.

Leading the group or not, stepping on the soldiers' feet was something he needed to be conscious of. He swore to himself silently and thought he needed to work on putting Weaver back in the driver's seat. Still, he was thankful Weaver hadn't done anything to shake up the dynamic.

The sergeant could have easily refused the instructions or, worse yet, caused a split in the group dynamic over small details. He waited for Weaver to turn back and flash him a thumbs up that they were ready to step off. He returned the gesture and watched the sergeant move down the hallway toward the utility room with Scott and O'Riley following close behind.

"Well, what are you waiting for?" he heard Kate say, waking him from his stupor of deep thoughts.

Luke looked down at the girl and grinned then glanced over at Tucker, who was adjusting the sling on his rifle. He dipped his chin at the soldier and stepped to the left, toward the front of the building. Moving down the path, they found that the hallway followed along the outer edge of the structure like a perimeter road, one narrow rectangle outlining a rectangular box. The building's design was more utility than creative.

The outer wall to their right was filled with tall, floor-to-ceiling windows covered in dark tint that still allowed in enough sunlight that the overhead fluorescent bulbs remained off. The rooms were all on the interior side of the hallway on their left and windowless, each having a solid, white steel door. They passed one of the locked doors every ten to fifteen feet, each marked only with numbers on the top center.

When they'd gone what Luke estimated was halfway around the building, he could see Weaver's team approaching him. He looked to the rear then back to the front and could see that they'd circled the entire building, finding every door locked. He was rethinking his original impression that this was office space. As Luke watched Weaver approach, the soldiers stopped to check doors. He observed the sergeant stop to turn a knob then pause and back away from the door.

Weaver pointed to Luke then to the door and grinned, showing his white teeth. He shot Luke a thumbs up and motioned for the others to join him. Luke moved quickly down the hall to Weaver's position. Unlike the other doors with random numbers, this room was tagged SYSTEM AND NETWORK ADMINIS-TRATION.

"Every room up to this point was locked up tight. All of them have weird numbers on the door with codes," Weaver whispered. "This one is different."

"Open it up then, let's give it a look," Luke said.

He nodded to Weaver, who turned the knob the rest of the way and pushed the door in. Lights clicked and popped to life, sensing the motion of the door. Luke swept in and to the left with the others filing in behind him, covering their own segments of the room. The space was brightly lit from the overhead lights and, like the other areas of the building, cool from the air conditioner. It was filled with a long and narrow, high-walled cubicle farm.

The open spaces were decorated with typical office furniture and government motivational posters. On a table was a half pot of coffee with a bloom of fuzzy mold floating on the surface of the dark liquid. Each cube held similar contents—computer monitors and paperwork covering cluttered workspaces, while desk calendars, framed photos, and fake plants personalized the spaces. Luke moved by them, knowing they could be searched for more details later. He held his rifle at the low ready and moved down the center aisle, peeking into cubicles as he passed.

He proceeded to the end of the room and held up short of a second door. This door had a keypad on it like the one outside, but the light on the pad was out, and the entry had been blocked with a chair, holding the door open. To the left of the door was a small desk covered with food wrappers and empty doughnut boxes.

He relaxed his grip on the rifle and waited for the others to close in. Back at the table, Luke pushed the garbage away to find a handwritten logbook. He picked it up and flipped through the pages. It was an entry log for what was called the *Server Console Room*. The last entry was over two weeks old.

In a trash can under the table were disposable paper cups and more candy and sandwich wrappers. Kate walked across the small space, discovering a plastic sack of candy bars and vending machine chips. She took out a candy bar and sat in one of the office chairs, working at the wrapper.

Luke looked over the space again and dropped the log back on the clutter-filled table. "A security team was guarding this door. They probably didn't have full access to the building, so they kept it propped open."

He spun and looked back at the space again. There was a black leather wallet on the table next to a stack of rechargeable radio batteries. He moved closer and flipped it open, finding a Virginia driver license for a man in his twenties and $60 in cash.

"They left in a hurry. Some rent-a-cop left his wallet and spare batteries for his radio," Luke said. He pointed at the door. "And then he forgot to pull that chair out and secure the space when they left."

"You can't know all of that," Weaver said.

"It's just a hunch, but if you have a better one, I'm willing to hear it. From this mess and the sacks, this place was being babysat by some low-rent security types. They chowed down on pogey bait and got fat in these chairs. They guarded this room, then my best bet is they were ordered someplace else in a hurry."

Weaver pointed at the door. "Why do you think it was open like that?"

Twisting his lips in thought, Luke shrugged. "Like I said, they didn't have access but still needed to keep eyes on it. Still needed to get in and out once the staff was cut loose. Or perhaps they were worried about a power outage or lockdown trapping someone inside, or them outside... who knows?"

Weaver nodded. "That makes sense, I guess. So what were they guarding?"

Luke shrugged and approached the door. He pushed it open and was hit with more of the cool, crisp air. This room was several degrees cooler and drier than the office space. As he stepped inside, motion-triggered banks of overhead lighting clicked and buzzed to life. The room was a large rectangle, half the size of the office space. But he could see through the windows lining the walls that they were overlooking several of the server rooms, which were in long rows in adjacent spaces. At the end of the narrow room was a large console with three large flat-screen monitors in a row. To the front of the displays, a single keyboard. Unlike the table and the cubes outside, this room was pristine, with no clutter. He moved to the console and pressed a key on the keyboard.

Clicking and buzzing, the monitors lit up, showing banks of status and alarm screens. He moved closer and tried to read what it was showing.

"They're system monitors. Basic shit, really," Scott said from behind him. "They monitor the health of the server arrays, hard drives, disc space, memory, stuff like that."

Luke stepped aside and let the Philadelphia soldier get closer. The man moved his hand over the screens, pointing out animated indicators. "It doesn't say what they do, but each row seems to relate to one of the rooms in this building. It's showing everything up and running. All of these servers are working normally." He took a beat. "Communications are also online." He paused again. "Luke, they are talking to someone."

Luke leaned in. "Talking to who?"

The young soldier shook his head. "I can't tell, could just be another bank of servers somewhere. But they are sending and receiving data."

"How do you know all this stuff?" Luke asked.

"I like computers," Scott said.

"Bullshit, don't let him shortchange you," Weaver

laughed. "This kid is a computer whiz. He just finished his bachelor's in computer science up on base and will be going to MIT to get his master's..." Weaver looked down. "Oh yeah. Well, maybe when all this shit is over, he will be."

Luke pointed at the keyboard. "Can you tell me if any of these servers control that radio tower?"

The young man pursed his lips and stepped to the keyboard. He pushed a key and a large login box popped up on the center of the three monitors. "Not without the log on credentials."

"You can't hack it or something?" Tucker asked, the soldier pushing in to get a closer look.

Scott shook his head. "You watch too much TV, Sergeant. Shit don't work that way."

There was a clack from the other room, and they heard a high-pitched squeak. Luke looked around the space. Everyone was in the small computer room, everyone but Kate. "Where's the girl?"

He turned back toward the door. Without thinking, he hastily stepped out into the cubicle farm. The room was empty. He heard the squeak again and raised his rifle. There was a click and clinking sound. He heard a familiar hiss and looked down. Feet from the toes of his boot lay a cylindrical tube. A flash bang grenade had rolled in and stopped just to his front, seemingly to taunt him for his error.

No time to react, he squeezed his eyes shut and said, "Well, this is gonna suck."

CHAPTER SEVENTEEN

DAY OF INFECTION, PLUS NINETEEN

North of Hayslette, Virginia

Gyles leopard crawled to the edge of the roof and rolled to his back, breathing hard. The roar of the infected trailed off behind him. He and Mega managed to get off the roof of the law office and jump to the next building without them taking notice, but the mass was growing by the minute. Gyles looked back over his shoulder, watched the crowd press in against the structure, and feared the building would implode from the pressure of the mob.

The fire from the alley was still growing, the flames glowing and black smoke drifting into the air. He lifted his head over the edge of the knee wall and looked out and down the street. He could see the next building's roof just below them. The buildings were set tightly together, lining the street with staggered roof lines. Taking a risk, he looked out over the edge and saw they were still a hundred feet from the next intersection. They needed to be on the roof nearest to it when Kenny returned with the rig.

He rolled away from the street side of the roof and moved close to the edge. Gyles swung his feet over the side and dropped the short distance to the next roof. He backed away with his rifle up and listened as Mega moved beside him. The soldier's fall was less graceful than his, the big man dropping with a loud thud. Gyles didn't bother to look back; instead, he ran the fifty feet across the roof, dodging vents and air conditioning units, to the next building. Before he hit the wall, he already knew the next roof would be too high. He reached up and found himself several feet short.

"Mega, get over here and boost me up," he barked.

The big man shook his head. "Boost me, Sergeant. No way your weak ass can pull me up there."

Gyles sighed, knowing he was right. He locked his hands and Mega stepped in, then Gyles hefted. The soldier grabbed the edge, pulling himself up and over the wall. After a moment's disappearance, he looked down and said, "Roof is clear." He then reached a gloved hand down to Gyles. Quickly, he was pulled up over the wall and onto the next roof.

They ducked down, moving slowly across the roof. At the center, they paused to catch their breath. Gyles looked in all directions. The roof they were currently on was the highest on the block, allowing them to clearly see the mob still focused on the law office. So far, infected hadn't figured out that they were on the move and no longer there. Looking deeper into the city, he could see the outline of the church's bell tower blocks away. Distant gunfire reminded them the occupants were still fighting for their lives.

"Kenny better come back with that truck," Gyles grunted.

"He is, Sarge. Come on, let's get to the corner; it's the next building."

Before they could move, there was a shudder in the building beneath their feet. Gyles looked back in time to see an explosion blast up from the law office. For a fraction of time, the mob were off their feet, scattered in the street. Then they became even more enraged, running back toward the building. Smoke began to billow up from the far corner then yellow flames licked up at the sky.

"What the hell was that?" Mega said.

Gyles shook his head and said, "I don't know. The fire must have hit a gas line or something."

Mega looked back. "This fire isn't going to help things."

"No shit," Gyles said as he pulled close to the edge and looked down. The drop wasn't bad, like on the previous buildings. He grabbed the edge then swung down. As he dropped, he looked up and saw the expression on Mega's face change to panic. He hit the ground and rolled to his back. Before he could rebound to his feet, Mega was firing.

Rolling to his side, he could see a group of infected leaving a roof access door. He kicked and scurried back. People in business suits were torn apart by Mega's machine gun. The soldier was screaming for Gyles to climb back up, but the roof's edge was far beyond reach. He turned and knelt, firing short bursts into the shadows to his front. His muzzle blasts lit the enraged faces of a crazed mob. They were screaming, their eyes fixed on him in anger.

He cut down two, then two more. A fat man in a double-breasted jacket, the blue sleeves torn, and his face already covered in blood came at him. A three-round burst tumbled the fat man back into the stair-well, taking others down with him. Soon, with both men firing, they had the group piled up in front of the access door. Gyles climbed to his feet and pressed forward, placing his shots into the darkness of the stair-well until the pile stopped moving.

Screams came up at them from the ground. He heard a slam and turned to see Mega climbing back to his feet. He had the feed tray open on his machine gun, slapping a new belt into the weapon.

"We've got to close that door, Sergeant," Mega said between gasps. "More will figure out that it's a way up."

Gyles looked at the bodies blocking the door, it would take too long to move all of them. He smiled out of the side of his mouth. "There ain't no closing it. How 'bout we just get rid of it?"

He snatched a frag from his belt and lobbed it just beyond the dead piled in the doorway then dropped to the rooftop. The explosion cracked, and debris rained down around them. He pulled back to his knees and tossed a second frag into what was left of the opening then dove for cover again. Another crack of thunder. This time the grenade had managed to destroy the walls of the access. The roof had collapsed into the stairwell and fire was spewing out of the openings in the debris.

"Great idea—now we got fire to the front and back of us," Mega said. "You are doing this shit on purpose, ain't you?"

Gyles looked out into the street. He spotted the big rig rolling in their direction, plowing through a sea of Primals. Kenny had failed to lose the mass of infected. "Fire is the least of our problems. Check that shit out."

"What are we going to do, Sergeant?" Mega gasped.

Standing up, Gyles changed the magazine in his rifle. The remains of the roof access were now fully engulfed in flame. The heat warmed his face and the smoke made his eyes sting and water. He lifted his arm, shielding his face from the flames. He could still hear the things screaming from within the enflamed wreckage, undeterred by the fire. On the street, the truck was moving closer; the intersection and east–west road were clear. Gyles watched as the big rig sped up. At this rate, the truck would be below them in seconds.

"Man, I can't believe they used to pay us for this shit, and now we do it just for fun."

"Fuck you, Sergeant, I'm not having fun," Mega shouted back.

Gyles laughed. "Come on, follow me," he shouted, running for the next wall. "Things are about to get exciting."

He moved around the perimeter of the roof, gagging from the acrid smoked. At the roof's edge, looking down, he could see the truck was now up on the sidewalk just inches from hitting the building. The tractor moved by them, not slowing. The horn began to blast.

"They ain't stopping, Sergeant," Mega yelled.

"Hell, nope, it don't look like they are." Without waiting to change his mind, Gyles planted his boots and jumped. Sailing through the air toward the box trailer, he knew he was coming in hot. He grunted, trying for a perfect parachute landing fall. Instead, he landed like a sack of laundry with pain at the impact of the painted plywood surface. He smacked his face and rolled to the edge, his boot catching on the aluminum framing.

He tried to stand and was knocked back down by Mega as the big man hit the trailer and bowled over him. The man's arms were flailing, searching for a handhold as he slid across the roof. Gyles reached out and caught the sleeve of his jacket. The fabric ripped, and he nearly slipped away before he found the soldier's wrist. Gyles planted his feet and tugged, stopping the other man's roll.

They were both on their backs, the trailer bouncing violently below them as it plowed through the infected that had taken notice of the big truck and were swarming after it. Gyles licked his lips and winced with pain, tasting blood. He pulled off his glove and felt his busted lip and blood pouring from his nose. He shook his head and tried to sit up, feeling off balance from the bouncing of the trailer. He reached out his hand and slapped Mega on the chest.

"You still with me, big hoss?"

"All day, Sergeant." The big man sighed. "Thought you said this was going to be hard?"

Gyles lay on his back, taking a much-needed breather. Suddenly, he felt the truck change direction. The bouncing smoothed, and the vehicle picked up speed. He felt along the roof to his side and found a large steel ring, probably used as a tie-down. He grabbed it with his hand and pulled himself to his rear. The truck was back on a main road, looping around toward the church. He didn't recognize the streets nor the terrain, but he could orient himself on the distant bell tower. His jaw dropped when he saw the infected all moving in the same direction. The Primals were on the parallel side streets and in yards, all of them running toward the church.

"Sergeant Gyles?" someone shouted.

He focused back to his front toward the cab. Culver was hanging out of the cab window, shouting back at him. He raised a hand, holding the small Motorola radio. "I got Sherman on comms. He's got people waiting for us at the garage."

No energy to speak, Gyles flashed a thumbs up and nodded. The man shook his head and shouted again.

"He says we better be ready to load up survivors because they're about to be overrun."

Gyles clenched his teeth and nodded his head, shooting another thumbs up. He could see the message was received when Culver returned the gesture and dropped back into the truck. Gyles reached to his hip and unsnapped his tomahawk. He looked over and pulled Mega up into a seated position beside him and held up the hawk.

"You still got yours?" he asked.

Mega patted at his side then pulled out his own hawk with a nod. "I got it; what's up?"

Gyles held the tool so that the spiked point was down, then swung hard and stuck it into the roof. He pulled up on the handle and the wood splintered out easier than he'd expected it to. He pushed away then looked back at Mega. "We need to make an opening before we start pulling those people off the church garage. No way we're opening those doors down there, so through the roof is the only option."

Mega grinned, spread his legs wide, and swung down with his own hawk, cutting clean through the roof. He twisted, popping a large chunk of the wood out. He changed his grip, swung again, and pried back, leaving a large hole. "Lucky for you, Sarge, breaking shit seems to be my specialty today."

Gyles smacked Mega on the back. "Good, stick with it. I need to move forward and figure this mess out."

The sun was now directly above their heads, the

heat of late morning blasting them. Looking to the front, he could see they were now making a wide turn. Ahead, Gyles spotted the opening to the alley. Kenny was a hell of a scout after all. He was bringing them right back the way they had come. A hundred yards past the opening to the alley would be the garage. The church wall was now visible over the heads of the infected.

The creatures had the church grounds surrounded, packed in tight on all sides. If the truck stopped in that alley they would swarm the semi, and Gyles didn't know what kind of horsepower it would take to get it moving again. He staggered to his feet and ran to the front of the trailer then yelled at the cab. Culver's head popped back out.

"Get close to that garage but don't stop," he shouted.

Culver nodded. "Way ahead of you. Joe is screaming the same thing. He says if we stop in that mob, he'll never be able to get us going again."

Exhaling hard, Gyles said, "Get me close to the garage. I'll jump over and talk to Sherman and arrange how best to get the civvies on board. You loop back around and start picking people up. Give me five minutes then head back for that alley."

CHAPTER EIGHTEEN

DAY OF INFECTION, PLUS NINETEEN

Mount Weather Emergency Control Center, Virginia

Luke opened his eyes to bright lights and squinted as the pain hammered down against his temples. He reached for his forehead and found his right arm restrained. He turned and struggled; his left hand was also strapped to his side, and his thighs and ankles were bound just as tightly. Swinging his head left and right, he could see he was dressed in light-blue pajamas, lying in a sterile white room with no furniture except the bed he was strapped to. He fought the restraints, arching his back and pulling, but the straps grew tighter with every tug. Soon he was flat against the bed, only able to move his head and his chest to breathe.

A door along the wall at his feet opened, and a pair of orderlies rushed in. A thick man held a syringe, the other was built like a whisky barrel, his short bulging arms holding more of the black straps Luke was already bound with. The men moved to his right side. He turned his head and shouted at them. "Stop! No, please —I don't need it. I'm okay."

The syringe-bearing orderly dressed head-to-toe in blue scrubs looked down at him and winked as his assistant forcefully slapped another wide strap across his chest.

Luke shook his head violently. "It's okay; I don't need it. Please just tell me where I am."

"Wait," a female voice called from the doorway. The orderly with the chest strap relaxed his grip and stepped away from the bed. The thick man held the syringe fractions of an inch from Luke's arm. His hand twitched like he was about to plunge the needle anyway. Then he pulled it back and stepped against the wall with the other orderly. The woman stepped into the room, her shoes clopping against tile with every step.

She was blonde with her hair pulled back into a bun. She wore a white lab coat over a black pantsuit. Luke blinked his eyes rapidly, trying to bring the details of her face into focus. "I'm okay, you don't have to do this," he said, his voice breaking with every syllable.

She stared at him, her palm still held up to the orderlies. "Deputy Ross. My name is Doctor Whitaker."

Luke looked at her hard. Taking in a deep breath, he tried to relax the strained muscles in his neck. "My name is Luke. I'm nobody's deputy," he said, gasping.

"But the uniform..." The woman forced a smile and looked down at the clipboard in her hands. Flipping a page, she said, "I see. We can cover that later."

Luke took his eyes off the woman, still blinking rapidly to clear his vision. He turned his head and focused on the syringe in the thick man's hand. The woman caught his gaze. "Lester, it's okay. Deputy Ross won't be requiring the sedative. Could you please leave us and send for Director Collingsworth, please?"

The thick orderly frowned and, without speaking, left the room. The squat man hesitated and looked at her, still holding the thick black straps. "Doctor?" he said holding one up. "Should I apply the additional restraints?"

She shook her head. "No, please don't. You can relax the others."

"Doctor?" the man said again. "He'll be able to move."

She waved a hand. "Yes, relax them, please; he's not infected."

The man nodded and moved to Luke's feet. Watching the man pull a lever, Luke felt instant relief in his thighs. Soon his hands and arms were loose enough that he could roll his shoulders. The man loosened the final strap on Luke's abdomen then looked at the doctor, who nodded, and the man left the room.

Luke eased his body against the mattress and looked back at the doctor. "Of course, I'm not infected." He adjusted his legs and tried to touch his face. Finding that he now could, he rubbed his forehead.

"I'm not bit. You had to have known that before strapping me down."

She forced another smile and avoided eye contact with Luke. "Yes, deputy—" She paused and said again, "Yes, Luke, we were aware that you were not bitten in our first examination, but you woke up earlier ranting and screaming. We had to take precautions." She looked back at the clipboard. "You were sedated and put in restraints."

Luke shot her a puzzled expression. "Earlier? How long have I been here?"

"A few hours," she said, not taking her eyes off the pages. "The medics tried to wake you, but as I said, you reacted violently." She stopped and flipped through the pages. "After the first attempt, we thought it best to let you awaken on your own."

Luke swallowed hard, trying to remain calm, knowing that everything he said would play a part in how he was treated here. "Where are my friends, the rest of my team?"

"They're fine," came a man's voice.

Luke looked at the door as a middle-aged man in a dark polo shirt entered. Unlike Doctor Whitaker, the man didn't wear a lab coat, but Luke could tell from a name tag that it was Director Collingsworth. The man walked across the room and stood next to Whitaker. He put out a hand, and she passed him the clipboard. "You took a pretty good shot to the head, Deputy Ross. How are you feeling?"

Before Luke could answer, Whitaker said, "He goes by Luke."

Collingsworth took a beat and frowned, studying the clipboard, then repeated the question. "How are you feeling?"

Luke looked at the man, then back to Whitaker. He could tell there was some tension between the two of them. "Who are you?" he asked, his eyes locked on the stranger.

The man smiled. "I'm Roger Collingsworth. I'm the Director of Security here, and I've had people tell me that you're a security risk."

Whitaker began to speak, but Collingsworth held up a hand, stopping her. "Deputy Ross, is there any reason that I need to be worried about you? Are you a risk to this facility?"

"You have my friends; what did they say about me?" Luke said.

"The soldiers?" Collingsworth snapped. "Like typical soldiers, they are refusing to speak. And the girl—"

"Kate? Is she okay?"

"She's fine," Whitaker said before Collingsworth could stop her. She drew a stern look in recognition of her outburst. She closed her mouth and nodded before taking a step back.

Collingsworth sighed and spoke. "The girl has plenty to say, but most of it is nonsense. She seems very troubled by whatever it is you have dragged her into."

At that, Luke laughed. "She's a refugee. I don't

know what happened to her, but she's all alone. I guarantee she's troubled." He paused to collect himself then looked back at the director. "What is it you want from me?"

"Why did you come here?" the man asked.

"Why did you attack us?"

Collingsworth grinned. "We watched you enter the camp. We would have approached you differently outside, but once you were inside the server room, we couldn't risk a fight or you damaging our equipment."

Shaking his head, Luke said, "If you watched us enter the camp, why did you wait for us to enter the building before talking to us?"

"It takes twenty minutes to open the doors," Whitaker said, drawing another cold look from Collingsworth.

The security man pursed his lips and put a closed fist to his forehead then nodded. "As my colleague just revealed, when the base is in full lockdown, it can take up to twenty minutes to open the blast doors. I assure you, we would have rather not caused a fight inside the server facility. Thankfully, your team felt the same way."

"Flash bangs and SWAT tend to do that to a person," Luke said, shaking his head. He glanced at Whitaker and could read the concern on her face. He knew he was doing this wrong. If he kept down this road, he'd end up sedated and strapped to the bed for a month. He took a deep breath and tried to relax. "Sorry we cut through the fencing. We couldn't be sure if the base was infected. We are coming from Camp Alamo. It's just east of here."

"Camp Alamo?" Collingsworth asked. "What's that? I've never heard of it."

"It's a survivors' camp, mostly refugees from Virginia. There's a batch of Marines and Seabees there, providing security. Well, at least they were."

The man looked to the woman then back at Luke. "When you say survivors' camp, you mean FEMA? But all of the FEMA sites are numbered, there are no names. The nearest camp is in Rochester, Camp 109."

"No, the Alamo is a military encampment. The Marines were on a fighting retreat from D.C. and they set it up when they realized they weren't going to find anything better. The highways are all blocked or bombed out, the infected are massing in—"

"Retreat from D.C.?" Collingsworth blurted out, cutting him off. "Retreat from what? D.C. is a stronghold. Every division the nation has to offer has been called there to shut down this outbreak."

Shaking his head, Luke looked down at his feet. "No, sir; the city and most every city like it has fallen. The Capital is gone." He exhaled. "Wait, how do you not already know this?"

The question caused Collingsworth's face to flush. "What we know is not your concern." The man took a step back, standing rigid, and passed the clipboard back to Whitaker. He turned and moved toward the door.

Spinning around, Whitaker said, "Sir, what do I do with the patient?"

He stopped in the doorway. Without turning he said, "You said he's not infected, release him to Quarantine B with the others. Keep him away from general until we get the all clear from command." Without waiting for a response, the man passed into the hallway and vanished to the left.

Whitaker moved back and closed the door before stepping to the bed to remove the already loosened straps. "You're lucky, you know. He could have kept you in here for up to a week without any reason at all. That's the standard protocol for people entering this ward."

"Then why the change of heart?" Luke asked.

"I think you struck a nerve with him." She moved around the bed and pulled the remaining straps from Luke's arms and chest. "We really don't know what's going on out there."

"Wait, this is like a command center. How is that possible?" Luke said. Sitting up, he rolled his shoulders and dropped his feet off the edge of the bed.

The doctor nodded. "We work in closed compartments here. I serve the medical department within the facility; Collingsworth, the security. If it doesn't pertain to our direct reports, then we don't know about it. We had some information about the riots and civil chaos in the Capital, and some disturbances out West. But once they closed the base, the information stopped."

Luke thought about the real reason they were here. "What about TV and radio?"

She smiled, knowing what he was getting at. "Yes, the frequency block also applied to us inside the facility. Everything RF, analog, digital, cell phones, everything is blocked. I heard a doctor in the burn ward say that some military-grade satellite phones were still working, but we haven't been able to confirm that." She looked back at the door behind her. "Listen, Luke, people in here want to know what's going on outside too. They have families out there, and all of us want to get home."

He frowned. "That's the thing, Doc. There is no going home, everything out there is gone. People are either dead or dying, and they have no way to call for help because of the damn jamming."

She held up a hand and leaned in close. "You shouldn't be talking like that, not here." Her voice changed to a whisper. "Most of Collingsworth's job right now revolves around maintaining that broadcast system."

"But why?" Luke said.

"When the orders came down to close the doors and activate the system, we were only at twenty percent capacity. Most of us thought that was a good thing. Usually, that would mean a drill or only a partial evacuation of the Capital. We've had lockdowns in the past that could last a month just to test the staff; you know, to make sure we were prepared for what this facility was designed for." She hesitated then said, "Plenty of the people inside still think that, but not everyone. Especially those of us in medical that have had contact with the evacuees from the city." She stopped and stared at the wall, in deep thought.

Luke looked at her hard. "Listen, doctor, I'm going to be real with you. If that jamming doesn't turn off, a lot of people are going to die."

"You didn't come here to look for survivors, did you?"

Luke closed his eyes and then opened them again. Whitaker put a finger to her own lips, silencing him. "Please let me get you checked into quarantine. Once there, you'll see that you're safe."

Luke sighed and went to stand, looking at his pajama-covered legs. He looked at Whitaker.

She smiled. "You'll get your uniforms back when we enter the quarantine ward."

CHAPTER NINETEEN

DAY OF INFECTION, PLUS NINETEEN

North of Hayslette, Virginia

The garage was ahead on the right side of the alley and coming at him fast. Gyles stood high on the front of the trailer, like a surfer, looking down the tightly packed space. Every inch of the alley was pressed shoulder to shoulder with the writhing Primals. Men from the garage's roof were firing down into the mass with little effect. A few would fall, but they seemed to be absorbed into the mass, which grew with every gunshot. Behind the makeshift picket line, on the garage roof, were groups of women and children huddled tightly with their belongings.

"This isn't going to work," Gyles said to himself.

He could see that if the semi slowed, the truck would quickly be overrun. They would have to make moving passes to get everyone on board that they could. He looked back and saw that Mega had a massive hole cut away in the top of the trailer. When Gyles asked what was inside, Mega told him it was only a few pallets of office supplies; there was plenty of room for stowaways.

Gyles waved at the cab, getting Culver's attention and shouted, "Bring it by the garage for a slow pass, but do not stop."

"No problem with that, Sergeant," Culver shouted back. "Old man up here says if he gets too slow, they climb the hood. He wants to head for the hills."

Gyles scowled. "He tries running, shoot him in the face."

Culver grinned. "We already had that discussion, boss. He ain't going nowhere we don't tell him to."

Looking up, Gyles could see they were closing in on the garage roof. "I'm jumping over to see if I can do something about this crowd. Loop back around and be ready to take on survivors."

Culver shot a thumbs up, and the man disappeared back into the cab. Gyles wobbled as the truck seemed to speed up then press right, the sides scraping on fences and trash cans in the alley. Joe was making it easy for him to make the jump. The garage was almost on top of them. Gyles compressed his legs and waited, as soon as the truck was in line with the corner of the structure, he took two lunging steps then jumped to the garage. As he sailed across the void, he saw women and children jumping to the truck.

He reached the roof and scrambled for footing as men pulled him up the side. "What are they doing? We weren't ready for them!" Gyles said, trying to catch his breath. He turned back to see the truck driving away. On the top, Mega had the people corralled on the roof and was guiding them into the hole in the trailer. Gyles looked up at one of the men who had helped him. "Did they all make it? Did anyone fall?"

A young man in a Detroit Tigers ballcap nodded. "They all made it, three women and four kids." The man pointed to a hole cut in the garage's roof; more women and children were filing out. "We'll get this group set up for the next pass."

Gyles shook his head. "We can't fill that truck, loading people seven at a time." He stood and looked behind him, into the church grounds. There were mangled bodies scattered along the lawns and walkways. "Are the infected inside the walls?" Gyles asked.

The young man looked down and shrugged. "Some demons have managed to get in, but the snipers in the tower are cutting them down. The church walls are strong. It takes a lot of them to get over the top, and when they do, the guys on the second floor kill them."

Having heard enough, Gyles made his way for the hole in the roof and spotted Zeke inside. "Where's Sherman?"

Zeke snapped around, hearing his voice. "Hey, soldier boy, looks like you held up your part of the bargain."

Gyles shook his head. "I haven't done anything yet. We have to get these people out of here. Where is Sherman?"

Zeke pointed toward the church. "He's in the sanctuary, trying to organize the withdrawal. We need to peel off shooters a few at a time or they'll breach the walls. Their gunfire is the only thing keeping them from rolling over the top."

Gyles bit at his lip. He already knew what needed to be done. He reached out and squeezed Zeke's shoulder. "That truck is going to keep making passes, but it can't slow down unless we clear this alley. You just get as many people on board as you can, you understand? As many as you can."

The old man forced a smile and dipped his chin. "You need help with something, son? You seem to have a plan."

"Nope," Gyles said. "No plan, just a stupid idea." He turned and walked across the attic of the garage and moved down narrow stairs into the workspace.

Two armed men stood by the door. As Gyles approached, one of them pulled back a bolt on the door. "The yard isn't safe, the snipers are killing them, but they can't see everything."

Gyles bit his lip and nodded. "Okay, what about the door on the other side of the yard?"

"There's men on it. In a minute, they're going to send a group across. If you want in the church, that'll be your chance." The man looked through a peephole then pulled back the door. "Here they come."

As soon as the door was pulled wide, Gyles stepped out and took up a position with his rifle at the low ready. On the ground he could see even more of the dead Primals in all conditions of dress, their bodies mangled by the gunfire. He kept his rifle aimed into the grounds as he ran toward the other door. At the halfway point, he crossed paths with a group of women carrying children. A young woman locked eyes with him. She was holding a baby to her chest. Gyles looked away, not wanting to remember her eyes.

"This isn't going to work," he whispered again.

He made eye contact with a man holding the church door. The man waved frantically at him, and he sprinted up the steps and flew through the opening as the man slammed the door and bolted it.

"You're going the wrong way, brother; this boat is sinking, and everyone is headed for the life rafts," the man said, looking at Gyles.

He ignored the man's comment. "Where is Sherman?"

The man frowned and pointed down the hallway. "In the sanctuary, organizing the withdrawal."

Gyles turned and moved down the hallway that was lined with women and children in single file, all waiting to cross the yard. He stopped and looked back at the man at the door. "Hey, buddy."

The man spun around. "Yeah?"

"You only putting women and children on that truck?"

The man shook his head up and down. "You got it, pal. Women and children first."

"Who the hell is supposed to protect them when that truck stops?" Gyles said. He turned and looked at the women in the line. "These ladies aren't even armed, why don't you just line them up and shoot them here?"

The man's jaw dropped, and he raised his hands in surrender. "Hey, pal, I didn't make the plan."

"I want an armed man or woman with every group of survivors. Make it happen. Do you understand?"

The man looked confused then stared at the women. He looked back at Gyles and dipped his chin. "I understand, I'll pass the word."

Gyles turned and continued down the hallway. At the end, he could see that the heavy wooden doors were open. Inside the sanctuary, there was chaos. Families were stuffing belongings into packs and moving into the hallway to join the line. He spotted Sherman standing with Lawson at the end of the room near the stairs leading to the bell tower. He moved quickly in his direction. Sherman spotted him and met him on the path.

"We're doing everything we can to evacuate everyone. I got people in the bell tower, working over the walls. Everyone else is fighting from the upstairs windows," Sherman said.

"It's not enough," Gyles replied. "Your guys are keeping them off the walls, but they'll get smart to what we're doing and rush the garage. We need to do more." Gyles looked around the sanctuary then back to Sherman. "How many do you have here? I need totals, including your fighters. How many passengers?"

Sherman looked back at Lawson. The man pulled

a notebook from his pocket and said, "About a hundred and sixty, give or take."

"Good, we got room for that. It won't be comfortable, but it'll work. I want you to do whatever it takes to get them onto that truck."

"Well, that's what we've been doing, but we've got a problem with Father Andre," Sherman said.

"I don't care about Andre; the truck is leaving—anyone that wants on it has a chance at survival. Leave the rest." Gyles sighed and lowered his head. He looked at the empty magazine pouches on his vest. "You can't get everyone here on that truck, dropping them on ten at a time. A few more passes and the alley will be packed so tight the truck will have to give up."

"This isn't sounding like a plan at all, son," Lawson said.

Gyles nodded. "You still have that radio?"

Sherman reached into a pocket and held it up.

"I'm going to the Humvee," Gyles said. "When I give the word, I need a pair of your guys to open the door and then for your boys upstairs to direct all of their fire on that gate."

"You're leaving?" Sherman asked.

"Did you see the fire downtown?" Gyles asked.

Sherman nodded. "Yeah, it's a damn inferno. The whole town will probably be on fire before the end of the night. Was that your handiwork?"

Gyles smiled. "I had some help, but yeah."

Raising his hand, Lawson interrupted. "What's the fire got to do with you leaving us?"

"I'm not ditching you," Gyles said. "We have a problem: these things are massed around this church too tight to get everyone out. And as Lawson showed me last night, there are other survivors in this city." He stopped and rubbed his tired eyes. "I know for a fact that these things are attracted to fire. I'm going to take my vehicle and lead as many as I can that way."

"That's suicide," Lawson said.

Shaking his head, Gyles sighed again, this time from exhaustion. "My Hummer is up-armored; nothing can get to me. I don't plan on dying, but that's what's going to happen to everyone living in this city if I can't draw those things away."

Gyles slung his rifle over his shoulder and moved out.

CHAPTER TWENTY

DAY OF INFECTION, PLUS NINETEEN

Mount Weather Emergency Control Center, Virginia

Luke smirked as a man handed him a white mesh bag with his uniforms inside. The attendant was on the older side of forty, dressed all in white with a Mount Weather patch on his right shoulder. The man caught his stare and looked at him, concerned. "Is there a problem?"

Shaking his head, Luke took the bag and dumped it onto a metal table to inventory. A set of black trousers, a black uniform top, blue T-shirt, socks, skivvies, and cleaned boots fell out. "Sorry, just not used to having such expedient laundry service."

The man nodded and handed Luke a receipt to sign. "If you have more, we can get it done for you pretty quick. We aren't even close to capacity in the laundry room," the man said, missing Luke's sarcasm.

Luke scribbled his initials on the receipt. "All my

gear is out there in my truck. You think they would let me go and get it?"

The attendant grinned and shook his head. "You know that isn't going to happen. They warned us that once we went underground, there was no going back until they send the all clear."

"Any idea when that might be?" Luke asked.

The man gathered up the empty bag. "If things continue to go as well as they are, maybe a couple more weeks." He put the signed receipt in a folder then held out a key and pointed to a far door. "You have been assigned Bunk 106. In the locker is everything you'll need while staying in the quarantine bay. Meals are served every four hours. You can dress here; the housing area is just beyond that door."

The man dropped the key on the metal table and turned, leaving out of the entry door. Luke dressed and took the key. He walked to the quarantine door and opened it. The space was long and narrow. Bunks lined both sides, with a numbered locker by each bed. Dining tables ran down the center of the room, and he could see people sitting at the far end. He looked to the left and saw a room labeled SHOWERS. He moved deeper into the room and looked at the first locker, labeled NUMBER 1. His key was 106. Yet all the bunks on this end of the bay were unassigned.

"'Bout time!" He heard a voice call from the end. Luke stepped to the side and saw Weaver headed his way. He was out of uniform, wearing a blue cotton jumpsuit. "What the hell happened to you?" the soldier asked.

Luke shook his head and sighed. "I don't even know." He nodded toward the end of the room. "You got food down there, or what?"

Weaver laughed and waved him ahead. When Luke was beside him, they walked together, and Weaver leaned in close. Speaking in a low voice, he said, "Bro, most of these people are clueless. They think this is still just a precautionary lockdown. They still think there are just riots in the Capital."

"I was getting that vibe, myself," Luke said.

Weaver turned and checked their surroundings. "This place is supposed to be for high-ranking government types, as high up as the President. Well, guess what? None of them showed up. That's why they still think it isn't real. People here are kind of pissed that they've been stuck underground for weeks with no news, while the big shots wait it out on the outside."

"The jamming?" Luke asked.

Nodding, Weaver said, "Yeah, it goes both ways. Apparently, this place has a top-of-the-line communications center, TV room, Internet lab—all the good stuff. But all of it is shut down, except for those with the highest levels of access."

"So at least someone knows the world has gone to shit."

Weaver shook his head as they approached a section of the dining tables. He turned and stood in front of Luke. "Nope, just like at the Alamo, all communications are being controlled out of some bunker in Colorado. Nobody here knows anything."

Luke looked over Weaver's shoulder to a group around the table. Several wore the same dark jumpsuits. He recognized the faces of his team, including Kate, but there were others that he didn't know.

Weaver leaned in close. "Stay cool around the strangers; I've been making friends. I think it's better that these folks are pissed off that they're locked up, with no word from the outside world, than having them depressed that it's all over."

"Why is that?"

"Thing is, for the people in here, they think we're all part of the exercise, like they're being tested. Even though the doctor and that security guys tells them it's real, it's not setting in yet. Probably because they can't see it." Biting at his lower lip, Weaver continued. "I know it sucks to lie, but if they think shit is dire with no place to go home to, they'll go into work mode and block us out. We need them thinking this is still just a drill, have them pissed off and wanting off this mountain. Just take some time; we'll chat when you get settled."

Waving his hand, Luke frowned. "No can do. Time is of the essence. You know what's going on out there, even if they don't. People are dying. We need to shut this down now."

"The bunker—all of it?" Weaver asked, his voice hesitant.

"No, fool, the jamming system. Nothing in that

225

jammer is vital to keeping these people alive," Luke said, moving around the man. He stopped and sat at the table, catching greetings from the others. Before he could ask about dinner, Kate was there, sliding a tray filled with food in front of him. He looked down at it. "You're serious right now? Steak and potatoes?"

She smiled and sat next to him. "This place can feed hundreds, but there is, like, nobody here. The cooks are actually complaining that they're wasting too much freezer beef."

Luke used a knife and fork and cut off a generous chunk of the steak and stuffed it into his mouth. "Let them complain away, this is damn good."

"Good, my ass," said a black man in a security guard uniform across from him. The clean-shaven man with short hair was younger than most of his own team. "There's a great place just down the road that has steaks twice as good. Seriously, if they'd just open the doors, I'd take you there myself."

Luke was about to correct him on the state of the world before remembering Weaver's warning. As far as the people in here were concerned, this was just an unnecessary precaution. Tucker laughed, breaking Luke's concentration. The stocky soldier was sitting half a table down with the rest of his team. "Man, stop bitching, Clive. The doors will open when they open. Just enjoy the free food for now."

"Free? Ha!" The guard grunted. "They'll probably take it out of my pay. And, hell, I got a wife and kid out there. She's probably tearing up some takeout while

I'm in here on lockdown. The woman hates to cook as it is, and if I'm not around, it'll be Golden Arches three meals a day."

Luke looked up from his steak and checked out the guard. Besides talking more than he appreciated, he noticed the man was wearing a Mount Weather patch same as he'd seen on the attendant's shirt. "Your wife and kid in here? Are they in the shelter?" Luke asked.

The man shook his head. "Hell, no. In town, man, I just said that. I don't rate high enough to have family privileges. Can't complain about it though; I knew the details when I signed up for this job."

"For someone that can't complain, you sure complain a lot," Tucker scoffed, and the other men at the table laughed.

"Why are you in here?" Luke asked. "I mean, in here with us tramps?"

Tucker stood up from the table and bellowed another laugh. "Go on, Clive, tell him why your silly black ass is in here with us."

The man smirked. "Guess I got lost out there. You know, when they sent the team to go grab you all up? Once you all were taken care of, well, on the way back I kind of drifted over to the base store. Thought it would maybe be open, and I could grab a six pack. Maybe use their phone to call the wife and check in. You know, they took all our cell phones? Anyhow, I figured I'd be back here before anyone noticed that I slipped off."

Luke shook his head. "And?"

227

"Damn store was closed. Hell, the entire base was closed and locked down like it was a holiday. I turned around and drove the truck right back to the security ramp. Got there just as the others did but guess ol' Collingsworth saw me on the cameras or something. He separated me from the group right off and ordered me into quarantine with you all."

"Do they think you're infected?" Luke asked.

The man laughed and shook his head. "Infected with what, fool?" Clive said. He stood and stepped back from the table. "Nahh... Collingsworth says it's protocol. Anyone separates from the group, anyone gets eyes off of someone, they get to spend forty-eight in quarantine." The man laughed again. "But I know he was just pissed. Guess I'm lucky he didn't fire me. He probably would have if this was a real lockdown."

Luke dipped his chin and looked right, down the table. At the far end were other strangers. "And who are they?" he asked.

Clive looked over his left shoulder and shrugged. "All different. Some got here late for check in. Others, staff same as me, did something to piss off Collinsworth, got themselves forty-eight."

Luke stuffed the last of the steak into his mouth, listening to the man drone on about how the security director liked to use the quarantine unit as his own personal holding cell. Luke nodded, following along, but once his belly was full, he was feeling the fatigue of the last two days. He looked across at Weaver. "Can you get me a meeting with this Collingsworth?"

Weaver shook his head and pointed at the entry door he'd passed through earlier. "That's locked up for the day. They take quarantine serious here, but that doctor of yours said she would be back first thing in the morning to check on all of us. I suggest you get some sleep, and we can hit him up in the morning."

Luke wanted to argue about it, but when he stood from the table, he could feel his thoughts already spinning, his head feeling light. A hot and cot was probably what he needed. The Alamo would have to wait another day.

CHAPTER TWENTY-ONE

DAY OF INFECTION PLUS NINETEEN

North of Hayslette, Virginia

When Gyles walked back into the church grounds, the scattered remains of the Primals had doubled. The moans and screams of the infected were prominent, coming from the back fence behind the garage. He watched as an infected man pulled over the top of the fence. There was a low-caliber rifle shot from somewhere on the second floor. The crazed man's head snapped to the side, then he rolled and crashed into shrubbery below.

Gyles unslung his rifle and watched the section of fence a moment longer before he moved into the yard with the pair of men Sherman had assigned to him. "The boys up there can shoot," he said to the pair behind him.

"It's Mr. Thompson and his three sons. Squirrel hunters."

Gyles nodded his approval. "I guess if you can pop a squirrel's grape from the top of a tree, shooting a crazy in the face is no problem."

He didn't wait for an answer and made a straight line for the Humvee. Before he could approach the door, he spotted Andre and his young assistant, Jacob, standing near the vehicle. Just behind them, looking very annoyed, was Zeke with his pistol in his hand, his eyes nervously scanning the yard.

"Father, you shouldn't be out here," Gyles said, moving past him and to the rear hatch of the Humvee. He popped the hatch and pulled out rucksacks, dropping them to the ground.

Andre moved by his side as he worked. He looked up at the bell tower. "I think we are more than safe out here. We have people looking over us."

Gyles went to go back into the truck and could see that Andre had moved into position, blocking him. He shook his head and stepped around him to the rear cab door, ignoring the man. He found a .50-caliber ammo box and opened it. Inside were several pre-loaded rifle magazines. After pulling the empties from his pockets, he replaced them with the fresh ones, filling all the pouches on his vest. He dropped the can and grabbed a canvas tool bag under the turret hatch then moved back to the rear of the vehicle. Andre was still blocking his path. Sighing, Gyles dropped the bag. "Okay, you have two minutes to tell me what you want, Padre."

Andre smiled. "I would like for you to reconsider this plan you have."

"Saving your ass?"

Andre held the smile and looked at the garage. "Of course, I can't keep people from leaving, but you want to evacuate the church. Is that really wise? Do you know what is out there?"

"We are already evacuating the church. You need to get your things and move with them," Gyles said, shaking his head in annoyance.

Pushing past the priest, he closed the hatch on the Humvee then pulled down one of the long radio whip antennas. He turned to one of the guards and asked him to hold the end. Digging through the canvas bag, he found a pair of road flares and a roll of green 100 Mile an Hour Tape, a versatile Army-issued duct tape. He quickly fixed the flare to the end of the antenna then took it back from the man and let it go up to its full length of nearly ten feet.

Andre again went to speak, but Gyles ignored him, repeating the procedure on the passenger side whip antenna. When he finished, he looked at Zeke and pointed to the ground. "These packs belong to my men. Can you make sure they get loaded on that truck?"

Zeke nodded. "Are you not coming back?"

Gyles shrugged. "Guess that's up to God right now. Ain't that right, Padre?"

Andre went to speak, but before he could, Gyles had turned to the pair of men. "I'm going to get right in front of that gate. I need you two to pop the flares on the antennas then open the gates. Sherman is going to give you as much support as he can from up there. I won't waste any time getting out. Make sure I clear the gates then lock up tight."

One of the young men looked at him, confused. Zeke stepped in. "Listen, Army, you go popping those flares, these things are going to go nuttier than a shit house rat. They'll be all over your ass."

Gyles nodded. "That's the idea. I'll fire the things up and make a loop through that alley and draw them back into the city. If this works, it'll clear out enough that they can stop with that truck and get you all out of here before the walls come down."

Andre laughed. "These walls won't fall."

Gyles turned, angry this time but holding back his rage. "It's broad daylight. As soon as the sun falls, there will be more of these things in the city than you ever knew existed. They'll climb those walls and pour over the top like a flood of death. I've seen it happen. Now pull your head out of your ass and save your flock!"

Stunned, Andre took a step back. Jacob put a hand on his shoulder, but the priest brushed it off. The man turned and walked swiftly back the church entrance. Gyles turned to Zeke. "Make sure you leave; don't let that man get you or your family killed."

"He'll come around; I know he will." Zeke asked, "And what about you?"

Gyles thought about it then heard the semi shifting through gears somewhere outside. "Don't worry about me. This thing is built like a vault. Just get everyone out of here, okay?"

Zeke nodded and extended his hand. Gyles returned the handshake and walked back to the driver's door. He shouted last instructions to the pair and dropped inside, closing the door tight, engaging the combat locks. He made a quick round of inspections and checked every door and the hatch. He then started the vehicle and spun it around in a three-point turn so that the nose was facing the gate. He looked in the mirrors and watched as Zeke moved back into the garage, dragging the heavy rucksacks. He looked at the face of one of the men, who shot him a salute. Gyles grinned and returned the gesture. He reached for a radio microphone on the dash.

"Sherman, you there?"

"I hear ya."

"Get ready, I'm about to piss off the neighborhood."

"We're ready. Good luck, and thank you."

Gyles looked out of his window and pointed at one of the men, then gave him a thumbs up. The man nodded, and he watched as the pair moved to the back of the Humvee and pulled down the long whip antennas and road flares. The antenna on the left popped to life and then the right. Gyles grabbed the wheel tightly in his gloved hands and eased the vehicle forward, his foot heavy on the accelerator. Then men moved into position by the gate and undid the lock. Immediately, the pressure of the infected outside forced it open.

While the men struggled to control the pressure,

Gyles pressed his foot to the floor. The Humvee rushed forward and blasted into the mob. At the same time, faces exploded as rounds pinged off the armor and into the crowd. The vehicle bogged down, the tires spun then found purchase and lunged ahead, crushing the bodies of the Primals under its wheels. He felt the Humvee surge with the torque of the engine then jump a curb. He smashed into a parked car, the small Honda being thrown up and into even more infected.

Daring a glance back in his mirror, Gyles barely saw the doors being closed as the mob turned from the gate and focused on the bright cherry flames of the flares. He gunned the engine again and cranked the wheel hard to the left, turning toward the back alley. The vehicle's momentum bogged down in the mass until the wheels shifted and he pressed through. He felt the curb and straightened the wheel, knowing he was on the road. Driving blind, he couldn't see anything through the mob, as they were pressed tight against every window. He snatched the handset back.

"Sherman, can you hear me?"

"Got you, soldier. They are on you like flies on shit," came Sherman's familiar voice. *"Even the ones from the front of the church are breaking off to follow you."*

"All good, but I'm having trouble navigating. I need you to tell me when to make the turn into the alley."

"I can do that... keep going; it's just ahead."

Gyles kept his foot hard on the accelerator, and the Humvee pushed ahead like it was buried in deep mud. He cringed every time it would bounce, find traction, and lunge forward. He knew it wasn't mud and rocks being ground under his tires. He made the mistake of looking left and saw a young woman's face pressed against the glass. Her eyes were blood red, every tooth broken. She screamed at him. He couldn't hear her over the others, but he imagined what it would sound like. His hands began to shake violently. Soon his legs were shaking with the fear-flushed adrenaline flooding his system. He was trying to control his breathing, concentrating on every inhale and exhale, when the radio squawked. *"Hard left now, soldier."*

Gyles cranked the wheel and waited for the Humvee to respond. He pressed harder on the accelerator, the vehicle bouncing and grinding ahead.

"Straighten it out. You're right on course."

He did as he was told and felt the pressure lighten as he entered the alley. The Humvee picked up speed and soon he could see the street ahead. Up above, he spotted the men standing on the garage roof, pumping their fists as he sped by, bouncing infected off the brush guard as he ran them down.

"It's working, dammit, it's working," Sherman yelled. *"They're all following you. We have a break in the alley; we're going to try and—"*

Gyles reached for the radio and tried to respond but caught static. He'd gotten out of the bubble; the jamming was back in effect. He looked at his hands, still intensely locked on the wheel. He was passing over the intersection where the pair of Primals had ambushed him earlier. He nearly crossed before cutting the wheel hard to the right, remembering that the road near the law office was blocked in tight.

The street ahead was open but the city block on his left side was engulfed in flames. He suddenly realized he was losing the mob and took his foot off the pedal, letting the pursuing mass close back in on him. He watched his speed, letting the monsters run alongside him. Sometimes, one would jump on the roof and reach for a flare. Others would climb the hood then roll off and be crushed by the heavy tires. He saw another intersection. Both paths straight ahead and to the right were blocked. Left was open, but it would take him right into the burning city.

He slowed and looked at a bearded man smashing his head against the bulletproof glass in his driver's window. "Hey, you want to go to a barbeque?"

The Primal's head reared back, and it smashed its face against the glass, its nose exploding, leaving a bloody smear. Gyles shrugged and made the hard turn left into the burning streets. "I'll take that as a yes," he said as the man rolled off the hood in the turn.

Buildings on the right and left were fully engulfed and for as far ahead as he could see. The wind was blowing in the direction of his travel, so he knew at least now the fire would spread away from the church. He slowed and looked in his mirrors and saw a sea of infected still following him, many of them with their clothing in flames after running frantically through the fire. Grinning, he again controlled his speed to stay just out of reach of the monsters chasing him. "Burn you, motherfuckers."

He looked up then slammed down hard on the brakes. The road ahead was blocked with another barricade, forcing him to press into reverse and speed backwards, losing his vision again when he collided with the mob. He hit a curb, losing control, and the Hummer skidded sideways then contacted a steel light pole that broke and fell over the Humvee, smashing against the hood. He shifted back to drive with the horde pressing against the vehicle.

The tires spun helplessly as he gunned the engine. He was pinned and surrounded, unable to move. Smoke drifted in through the vents with the cool air of the air conditioner. He removed his gloves and touched the steel plating, feeling the heat radiate back at him.

A man with a burnt face and singed hair screamed at him through the side window while others climbed onto the hood, beating at the bulletproof windshield. "Well, this really sucks, you guys," Gyles said, yelling at the Primals. "I invited you all to a party, and then I get stuck on the way there."

After cutting the engine to avoid drawing in more smoke, he crawled into the back of the Humvee, ignoring the screaming mob. He tossed aside the ammo cans and boxes of MREs, until he found the five-gallon plastic water jug he was searching for. He dug through his pack and found his poncho liner, which he soaked with water before pulling it over his shoulders. In a medic pack, he found a foil space blanket and covered himself with it. Several minutes later, the frequency of the vehicle being banged and rocked with the impact of the Primals began to slow. He peered through a gap in the armor and saw that the flares had gone out.

The Primals were moving away. No longer able to see him, they were being drawn farther into the burning city by the blazing fire around him. He strained to see the nearest building was in flames. Through the vehicle's armor, he could feel the heat and hoped the Humvee would survive; he really didn't want to burn inside, or become dinner on the outside. He reached for the jug and splashed more water on his face and took a long drink. Then he felt the last of the Primals stop their banging and move away.

"Well, boys, I know you all want to play, but Sergeant is tired. I just want to take a quick nap, if that's okay with you all," he said as he dropped back against his rucksack.

The heat of the armor burned on his face like he was staring at the sun. He could hear the infected outside screaming—not from the hunt, but from the agony of being cooked alive. He put his hand back on the skin of the armor. It was warm, but not so hot that it burned him. He was exhausted and had nothing left to give today. Gyles shrugged and poured more water over his head. He lay back and closed his eyes, wondering if the people in the church made it out.

CHAPTER TWENTY-TWO

DAY OF INFECTION, PLUS TWENTY

Mount Weather Emergency Control Center, Virginia

The lights flashed on with a loud metallic click. Luke startled awake, staring up at the ceiling. He heard groans from the other bunks and the clanking of a door at the end of the large bay. He looked at his watch, it was just after 04:00.

"Damn, they don't sleep late here," he mumbled as he sat up and rolled his legs off the bed, letting his bare feet rest on the cold concrete floor. He watched as carts rolled and squeaked across the floor, filled with breakfast trays. They stopped at the tables and started passing them out as residents staggered over and sat down.

Luke turned his head when he heard the familiar clopping of heels on the cement floor. Doctor Whitaker was walking with two men in the security uniforms. She carried a bundle of folders under a wooden clipboard. At the edge of the dining tables, now filled with the residents, she stopped and began reading names. Some, she said, were released, others she instructed to go to examination rooms. She looked over and made eye contact with him briefly before turning away.

As the doctor continued to read the names, Luke stared at her.

"Cassie Smith, exam room one. Alex Burns, report to maintenance. Hanna Jones, report to science. Jeremy Clive, return to duty—"

"Hold up on that," a security guard interrupted. He pointed at Clive, who was sitting at the table, shoveling scrambled eggs into his mouth. "Clive, grab your gear and stay with us. The director wants an eye kept on you."

Clive shrugged and continued eating. The doctor turned and glared at the guard for interrupting her. She continued reading the names. Luke's ears perked when he heard his team's names, followed by his own. "... Luke Ross, exam room six."

Then she looked at him again and continued past the dining tables and through a door at the end of the dorm that Luke hadn't noticed the night before. He looked up as Weaver stopped beside him. The man was out of the coveralls and back in his Army uniform.

"What's going on?" Luke asked.

Weaver shook his head. "They did this yesterday right after we got checked in. They gave us full medical exams then brought us into a room and asked a load of questions. We all stayed pretty quiet, but Kate was blabbing about monsters and you saving her in the refugee camp." He laughed. "I'm pretty sure the doc thinks that little girl is crazy."

Luke grunted. "Because she's the only one telling the truth."

Shrugging, Weaver laughed again. "Exactly. I told you these folks aren't ready to hear that stuff. Last they heard was riots in the Capital, then the lockdown bell rang. Most of these new folks don't even know what's going on or heard from friends and family. Plenty of them are just diplomats and were evacuated at the request of some senator. They've been waiting here until the facility can figure out what to do with them."

"So, they really have no idea?" Luke asked.

"Talking to Clive, we're the first people to be let inside since the gate was closed."

"The doctor knows, and that director, and whoever they report to knows. They knew about the infection and activating the jammer; they just aren't telling everyone for some reason."

Weaver looked over at the food. "Well, we're about to find out soon enough. Grab some chow, and I'll meet you in the exam room."

After the soldier moved away, Luke grabbed a shower bag that had been provided with the locker and his bunk. He made his way past the dining tables and to the latrine, where he stayed quiet, listening in on the conversations of the strangers.

Weaver was right in his assumptions. There was a woman and her daughters who had flown in from

Europe just two days before the borders were closed. She was the wife of an ambassador, being held in quarantine until her husband arrived. She hadn't heard from him in two weeks. A man from Pennsylvania said he was an expert advisor to a White House staffer who still hadn't checked into the facility. Luke moved up to a shaving mirror and was flanked by a thin man with a bulging beer belly. He had tribal tattoos covering his sunburnt arms.

"You came in with the soldiers. Nice to have friends inside," the man said without looking over.

Splashing his face with water and applying shaving cream, Luke nodded. "Yeah, just yesterday." He glanced at the man in his peripheral vision. He had scars on his neck and shoulders and didn't fit the diplomat profile. "What about you?"

"Yeah, three days ago."

Luke turned. "I thought nobody has come in since the doors were closed."

The man grinned. "Nobody has come in through those doors maybe. I came in through the west branch. I'm a helo pilot."

Looking at the man's long, unkept hair, Luke shrugged. "You don't look military; who do you fly for?"

The man looked at him sideways. "C.N.R.T. Just shuttled a crew here from another facility. Waiting for this doctor to clear me so I can grab another mission." He stopped and looked at Luke's folded uniforms on the bench, the black cargo pants on the top of stack.

"Aren't you with the Nert also? I figured the uniforms and all."

Luke forced a grin. "First rule of Nert, right? Don't talk about Nert," he said laughing.

The man chuckled. "Exactly, you never really do know; they're taking all sorts these days. What are you doing with the response teams then? Rescues? Escorts?"

Luke shook his head. "Anything to make a dollar, you know. I'm hoping I can get a new gig myself. That last thing in D.C. was tough."

"Shit, you ain't lying—jobs are getting shittier by the minute. I was sent to bring some woman back from Arlington. Got there, and she was dead, her security team all turned. Barely made it out of there my own damn self." The man splashed water on his face and wiped it with a towel. He dropped back to a bench and began dressing. He put on a pair of black cargo pants, and a black utility shirt over a white T-shirt. "You know, if that director tries to send you east, tell him no thank you. Nothing but death that way. Get out to the Rockies or Texas, if you can."

Luke moved to the bench and dried off. "Any news on Fort Knox?"

The man shook his head. "Nope, they're doing their own thing, just like Michigan and the Midwest states. Nert can only offer help, can't force them to take it."

"I hear that," Luke said, pulling on the long pants and lacing his boots.

The man quickly stood beside him and extended his hand. "Hey, you ever need a pilot, ask for me, Aaron Jones."

Luke returned the man's handshake. "Luke Ross. I'll do that. Safe travels," he said, watching the pilot walk away. He looked back in the mirror and grabbed up the rest his gear and put on his sheriff's deputy shirt. Things were going sideways fast if the government was taking contractors like Jones. The man was friendly enough, but he wasn't the government type and too free with his information to be a professional. If Luke had to guess, they picked him up at the end of a bar.

He left the restroom and walked by the carts filled with breakfast. He grabbed a biscuit and a cup of coffee and moved to the exam rooms. He found room six with the door open and most of his team already inside. The space was shaped like a classroom, except instead of desks, it was filled with a long white table surrounded by chairs. Benches lined the outside walls. He walked around the table, to the end of the room, and sat on a bench.

Just as he looked up, the door closed. Doctor Whitaker was inside with the two security guards, one with a red cap and a thick, black mustache. Behind them, they were joined by Clive, who was now back in full uniform. The doctor went to speak, when there was a knock at the door. Clive reached back and opened it. He stepped aside, and the director entered. He looked around the room, inspecting faces, then sat at the head of the table.

He cleared his throat and then spoke. "Doctor Whitaker, any issues to report?"

She shook her head. "No, sir, they're all cleared. I see no reason to further hold them in quarantine."

With a nod, he reached toward her, receiving a folder. He placed it in front of him and opened it, removing a type-written page. "I'm prepared to offer each of you a position. Being military and law enforcement, the security team would be the best—"

"You need to shut down the jamming," Luke said, cutting him off.

"Excuse me?" the man said.

"People are dying out there because they can't communicate. There's a military base being overrun. They can't get support in or out from the airfields because of the jamming. We need to shut it off."

The director smiled, his lip twitching nervously. "There is no jamming."

"Shut it off," Luke snapped back.

The man snarled and repeated, "There is no jamming. We broadcast an emergency message and instructions to the people by the President's order. Only the President can order it to be turned off."

Luke shrugged and looked at his men. "If the President hasn't shown up by now, he's probably dead. Washington is a ghost town now—only the Primals live there."

"You liar," the director shouted.

Luke had finally struck a nerve. He could see the guards' posture stiffen. Clive looked confused, and the doctor's hands twitched nervously. Luke watched as the guard with the red cap gripped the handle of a taser.

Shaking his head, Luke said, "There's no reason to lie in here, pal. What would I have to gain? All we want is to give the people out there a fighting chance. We know about the people in Colorado calling the shots, the communications window, and that half the East Coast is wasteland. You don't need to sugarcoat the shit for us. People are dying out there because you have the radios shut down, and we can't get instructions to them."

"Now, just wait a minute," the director said, holding up a hand. "That is not what's happening."

Luke stood. "No. We don't have minute; people are dying right now. Maybe it was a good idea to give the media a time-out when things were frantic, but that's over. Now turn the communications back on."

The director's hands were shaking, the paper held between his fingers rattling like a leaf. "There is no jammer."

Luke sat back down and leaned against the wall with his arms crossed. He could see the shock in Clive's and the other guards' faces. They had no idea— this was all new to them. Whitaker looked away and avoided eye contact. He smirked; she knew about the radio interference. To the director, he said, "I'm not interested in taking a security position with anyone jamming the voices of people just trying to survive. I'd rather take my chances outside."

Slamming the paper to the table, the director rose from his chair. "Very well then. I am not running a prison, here. I have no obligation to shelter you. I want you out of my facility, now." He turned to one of the guards and said, "Give these people back their equipment and return them to the gate. If they come back, shoot on sight—and no more trespassers, or you can pick a replacement." Then he turned and stormed out of the room.

Weaver stood up and stretched. "Well, I think that went well."

Luke looked at the faces of his team. They were all smiling. For a moment, he thought he might have made a mistake, playing his cards so hard—they may have preferred this steak-and-potato hideout—but now, looking at their grins, he knew he'd made the right choice. That, or they just appreciated a good show.

The red hat guard shouted, "You heard the man. You've got five minutes to grab your shit, then we're walking you all on out of here."

As Luke moved toward the door, the doctor stopped him. "Can we have a word?"

Luke shrugged. "According to Mister Mustache, I got five minutes to burn."

"Are you sure about the jamming? Is it really having that effect out there? We were told it was to keep populations controlled so the C.N.R.T. could manage the response to the infection by controlling the message and delivering all instructions. I mean, we were told it's working."

"C.N.R.T... What exactly is this 'Nert' I keep hearing about?" Luke asked, answering her question with a question.

"They are the command for the response. The Coordinated National Response Team, to be exact. They are running everything. Put in place by the President once things went critical, they're running everything from the FEMA camps to finding a cure for the infection. Everyone in the national government reports to them."

Luke shook his head. "Well, they're also blocking military communications, preventing units in the field from getting help. Preventing Camp Alamo from getting the air support they need. Hell, our trucks can't even talk to each other over long distances. We don't even know how many survivors are left out there because nobody can call for help. Local radio stations are even blocked."

"No, that's not right," she said, "That's not what the interference is. It's just an override. The emergency broadcast has been playing twenty-four hours a day with instructions since all of this started."

"No, ma'am, just clicks and beeps. Radio, cell phones, all of it. You put us in the dark."

Her mouth opened, and she looked down at the floor. "I had no idea."

"Well, you do now. If you have any say in it, get the jamming shut off." He went to step away but before he did, he looked back at her. "You know, if we can't kill it the nice way, the Marines are going to eventually roll up here and blow it all. Secret is out, lady. We all know what's going on here." He grinned. "And I know the Marines. They won't care what they blow up with it. Not sure you all want that." He didn't wait for an answer and moved into the hallway to join the others.

Weaver was waiting for him by the exit door, smiling. "Sweet words goodbye?"

Luke shook his head. "Something like that."

Red Hat was waving his hand, and Luke and the team followed him and the other guards through the exit door and into a long corridor. At the end was a pair of elevators. Both opened at the same time. Luke stepped into the one on the right with Clive, Weaver, and Kate. Red Hat and the others went to the left. Looking at the wall, Luke could see there were no call buttons. The doors closed, and the elevator began to rise. Clive moved close to him. "You know, brother, not everyone is happy here."

Luke nodded. "I can imagine."

Clive moved toward the wall and turned so that his head was away from a corner camera. "We signed up to survive World War Three, not World War whatever this shit is. If things are that bad out there, I'd rather get out and find my family."

Seeing that the man was sincere, Luke turned away from the camera. "Things are that bad out there, and a lot more are going to die."

"What can we do?" Clive said.

"We need to stop the broadcast."

Clive smiled. "I don't know anything about that

broadcast, but you take me with you. I can get you onto the main floor. The first deck," he said, pinching his key card. "There's lots of computers and shit up there. During training they said that's where all the messages would come in and out to the facility; where they would give instructions to people."

Before Luke could answer, the elevator stopped and the doors opened. They stepped out and were at another long corridor. The walls and floor were made of poured concrete and painted white. Red Hat barked at them and pushed them ahead, into a large storage room filled with lockers and large black storage bins. He pointed. "All your crap is in there. Your weapons too, but we got your ammo. We'll give you that back when you leave the seal."

The team checked the bins, and just as they were told, they found all their equipment. Luke grabbed his police tactical vest and dropped it on. The others strapped into their body armor and put on their packs. All the while, Red Hat barked at them to hurry up.

"Where next, tough guy?" Luke asked.

The man stepped into Luke's face and scowled. "Air lock. We got about a twenty-minute wait for the doors to open and get you all topside."

"What if I have to piss?" Weaver said.

Red Hat spun. "Then you better hold it. Now move, I'm tired of you already. Can't wait to get you out of here."

When they stepped back into the hallway,

Whitaker was there. She called Red Hat by name then pointed to Luke. "Carl, I need to speak to him again."

"But ma'am, the director said—"

"It's fine, Carl," she said, this time with less patience in her voice.

Luke smiled. *"It's fine, Carl.* Damn, he just got punked."

Carl shook his head and stepped away, surveying the space. "Hey! Where the hell did Clive go? That kid is always running off." He looked at his watch and cursed, bunching the soldiers and Kate together. Tapping his watch impatiently, he looked at Whittaker.

She walked Luke a short distance down the corridor then stood with her back to the security guard. "We've heard rumors about what is going on, but nobody wanted to believe it. Even Collingsworth doesn't know the extent of what's happening out there. We're in the dark also... the clicks and beeps, as you said. If people were alive, we should be able to talk to them, to doctors in other bunkers. We should able to call others for assistance, even pick up outside news stations. Everything went dark, just like you described. The director said it was part of the protocol, but it's never been part of the training."

"Help me shut it down," Luke said.

She shook her head. "Some people in the science lab have been working on something, but we have no way to run it. The lab isn't connected to the larger network." She reached out a hand as if to shake. When

Luke returned the gesture, he felt her pass a tiny thumb drive. "Get it into any of the main subsystems, and it'll do the work."

Luke rubbed his chin and nodded. "What's going to happen?"

"It'll start an internal clock. You will have ten minutes, and the mainframe will reboot. When it comes back online, the broadcast code will be corrupted. The interference program won't restart with the rest of the systems."

"And doctors did all of this?"

She smiled. "No, our IT guy helped design many of these systems, including the President's broadcast; he knows how to break them. One more thing, when the mainframe cycles, everything will go dark. You have to be out before they come back up."

"How long to wake up?"

"Just a few minutes," she said. "Sorry we can't help more."

He slipped the drive into his front pocket. "We'll try and get it done."

"Luke, don't kill anyone... they don't know," she said then turned and walked away from the group.

Red Hat was on him before he could respond. "Let's go, we're way behind schedule."

Following the man's instructions, he fell back into line with the group and marched down the long hall-way. At the end was another set of double doors. Above them were enclosed light bulbs of yellow, green, and red. The first guard opened the door as Red Hat pushed them through. This time, instead of an elevator, they turned and walked up the left side of a ramp made of poured concrete. The walls were lined with more of the enclosed light bulbs. On the other side, they could see workers moving back and forth while, down the middle, golf carts drove past.

Luke could see large numbers painted over doorways. The one they'd just left was 3, and they were headed toward 2. Each door had a card reader like the ones they'd seen outside. He increased his pace so that he was next to Weaver. "We can do this, but it has to be done before they get us outside."

"You have a plan?"

Luke shook his head. "No."

Weaver pointed at the end of the ramp. There was a large vault door. Just to the left of it was an entry door with the stenciled number 1 over it. "I think we're running out of time."

CHAPTER TWENTY-THREE

DAY OF INFECTION, PLUS TWENTY

Mount Weather Emergency Control Center, Virginia

They were lined up against the wall while the enclosed bulbs flashed yellow. Red Hat kept checking his watch. Looking at the vault, Luke watched the twenty-five-ton blast door set on pneumatic hinges move fractions of an inch at a time. The level-one door was just across from them, but in between was Red Hat and his guard force, which had now doubled.

An electric golf cart sped up the ramp, bright lights flashing as it approached. Red Hat turned and looked toward it. "Who the hell is that? Nobody is supposed to be out of their assigned areas when the seal is breaking." He pointed to the flashing yellow lights. "Are they color blind or just stupid?"

The cart stopped just feet away, and two men got off, leaving the bright headlights of the cart still lit. A large black man in a security uniform stepped from the driver's seat and walked around the back then dragged another man from the cart on the passenger side. Red Hat took a step closer and said, "Richardson, is that you? What the hell are you doing on the day shift?"

"Found this fool for you," the man said, pushing Clive forward. "He was trying to sneak back into the barracks."

Carl shook his head. "Where in the hell did you run off to this time? You know the director is going to fire you for this. You'll be working in the kitchen for the next fifty years," he said, laughing.

Clive raised his hands in surrender. Red Hat moved in closer, sneering at him and still making his threats. As Clive's hands came back down, he threw a right hook that caught Carl on the jaw, knocking the man out. The other guards reached for their tasers, but before they could, the big man, Richardson, pulled an M9 service pistol and had it pointed at them. "Don't make me kill you fellas. We just want to leave with these gentlemen. None of you all need to get hurt."

The guards raised their hands and Clive ran at them, slapping on cuffs and turning them to face the wall. The big man moved back to the cart and killed the lights. He reached inside and pulled out a large canvas bag then tossed it to Weaver. "Ammo is inside. Best you all get loaded up. This won't go unnoticed."

Weaver nodded and accepted the bag, unzipping it. The pack was full of loaded magazines. He took a stack and loaded up his vest before passing it to the others. Luke walked past them and stopped at Clive, pointing at the large, stenciled number 1 over the small steel door. "Can you still get me inside?"

Shrugging, Clive said, "Sure, but like I told you, I don't know anything about those systems. Unless you know what you're doing, I don't see how it'll help."

Luke pointed at the vault. "Do you know anything about that? How much longer before it's open?"

Clive turned and looked at a control panel and a meter next to it. Like a gauge, it showed minutes on the bottom and inches and feet on the top. "Enough to get a man through in about eight minutes, a truck in fifteen."

"A man will do." Luke turned toward the first-deck door. Weaver handed him a stack of large magazines for his AR-10 rifle. Luke took them and dropped three into the front pouches on his vest, and another two on each side. He looked at the big man. "Richardson, is it?"

"That's right."

"What will their response be? Someone has to be coming."

"Yes, sir, SWAT is probably dressing right now. Then they'll be rolling up this ramp. Whether they shoot or ask questions will be up to the director."

Luke turned to Weaver. "Hold the line here. But try not to kill anyone if we don't have to."

Weaver dipped his chin and pointed to the entry door. "You get that done, and I'll take care of this."

Clive moved around the pair to the card reader and

swiped his badge. After entering a series of numbers into the door's keypad, the door clicked open. He pulled the door back then snapped an arm at the top, sticking it into the open position. "Those guys will get wise and lock everything down soon; we don't want to be sealed in when they do," Clive said, looking at Luke.

"What about the vault?" Luke asked.

Clive shook his head. "Nope—only thing that can stop that door from opening are these controls or the power going out."

"Any other way outside?" Weaver said.

Clive pointed back into the facility. "There is another door at the back of the complex, but if they hadn't already started the opening sequence we'll be out before they are."

Luke took a breath and waved his hand into the first deck. "Lead the way then."

Clive drew his own service pistol then stepped inside. They were moving fast down a narrow hallway. Like the others, this one was sterile, with white walls and smooth concrete floors, no photos or framed pictures. There were doors every few feet with placards over them. Several were empty, as if the spaces were waiting to be occupied. "Where are all the people?" Luke asked.

Clive shook his head and turned a corner in the hallway. "Protocol. When the seal is opening, you are supposed to stay at your desk or in your quarters." He took several more steps then stopped again. He put his hand on a door and looked back at Luke. "The IT guys and network people for the facility all work in here. I'll distract them while you do what you need to." Clive put his shoulder to the door, ready to rush in. "You ready for this?"

"I'm good," Luke answered.

Clive shoved the door open and rushed inside, yelling. Luke wasn't prepared for the outburst; the guard was screaming that they were under attack and telling the workers to move to the back of the room, that he would protect them. People fled workspaces. Some cowered and others tripped and fell as Clive ran at each of them, screaming for them to move. Clive ran halfway down the room then took a knee, with his pistol aimed back at the door.

Stunned, Luke stood in the doorway for a second before stepping inside, where a dozen workers cowered at a back wall of the large computer lab. Clive was still screaming at them to cover their heads and look away. Stifling a grin, Luke began moving through workspaces, trying to find one that looked important. He finally stopped at a long, U-shaped desk with a number of monitors that mirrored the console in the building outside. He searched for a place to insert the drive, finding a slot at the edge of a keyboard. Once the drive was inserted, a box popped up on the center monitor and just as quickly vanished. He looked at the desk and moved a stack of papers to cover the inserted thumb drive, then back at the monitor.

"Is that it?" he said to himself. He looked at his wristwatch and set a timer for ten minutes. They had just enough time until the lights went out. Before he could tell Clive he was done, gunfire echoed from the hallway. The workers started screaming again. Luke turned and yelled, "They need backup, let's go."

Clive shot a salute then turned to the cowering workers. "Hey, you all stay here until we get back—no matter what, don't touch nothing or go into that hallway," he said before turning and running back toward Luke.

Once they were outside the door, they ran down the hall, back to the entrance. There was gunfire and rounds popping off outside. Clive stopped him. "Did you do what you needed to get done back there?"

"We're about to find out," Luke said. He looked over at the vault door. It was still creeping open, probably already wide enough for Kate to get out. In a few more minutes, it would be enough for Richardson. He stuck his head out and could see his men taking cover in alcoves along the walls. On occasion, Weaver would reach out and fire rounds into the roof. Return fire would come back, pecking at the concrete and pinging off the blast door. Luke turned his head down the ramp, where a row of SWAT members were creeping up behind bulletproof shields.

"Shit." He looked at his watch then yelled out, "Hold your fire! Hold your fire!"

Weaver gave him a thumbs up and leaned back into the alcove. When Luke looked back around the corner, the SWAT team had stopped its forward movement. "We just want to leave!" Luke yelled.

There was silence from down the ramp. Weaver went to look out, and there were gunshots, rounds peppering the corner of the wall, inches from his friend's face. Luke yelled again. "What the hell? I told you... all we want to do is leave."

"I was letting you leave." Luke recognized the director's voice. "What is wrong with you? You attack my guards, you break into my communications lab."

Luke looked at Clive, and the man shrugged. "Cameras, brother, they see everything."

"You're right. We had to try, but we couldn't find anything. We just want to leave," Luke shouted. He looked at his watch; they were down to five minutes. The vault was now wide enough for them to leave. But his people would be cut down if they tried in front of the firing squad on the ramp.

Daring a look around the corner, he could see the SWAT line and several men with their rifles pointed at him. Just behind them was the director and a group of guards. One of them was on the phone. The man turned to the director. "He's telling the truth, sir. The lab says they didn't do anything, just scared the piss out of the systems administrators. Sounds like they heard our shots and got the hell out of there."

The director turned away, then looked back up the ramp. "I could have you locked up for a decade for this."

Luke let his rifle hang from the sling and put his hands up, stepping around the corner. "If we start a real firefight, shit is going to get ugly fast—my people go back to that lab and kill them all or burn it down," Luke said. "I told you, all we want to do is leave."

The man next to the director leaned in close. They talked, then the director took a step back, waving his hands frantically. "Go, get the hell out now."

Luke turned to Weaver and pointed at the vault door. It was now wide enough for them to easily walk through to the other side. Weaver pointed to Tucker and Kate. Apprehensively, they left their hiding places and slipped out, followed by Scott and O'Riley. Richardson and Clive peeled from their spots and went through the opening with Weaver.

Walking backward toward the door with his hands still up, Luke checked the ramp space a last time. They were all out. He turned around and exited through the vault door, where his people were waiting. Clive and Richardson were working to open a smaller, manual set of blast doors as the rest of the team covered them. In no time, the small door opened, letting in bright daylight, and Luke's people poured out. The vault door made a loud clunk then the direction reversed, slowly closing. Before it moved a full inch, the lights went out.

As Luke heard the SWAT team cursing from the other side of the door, he turned and ran after the others, into a large parking lot. The structure behind him looked like little more than a garage from the street. Richardson was sprinting toward a white-and-black painted Suburban with the others close behind him. Weaver was halfway in between with his rifle pointed back at the building.

Weaver's expression changed just as gunshots and rounds zipped past Luke's head as he ran. Weaver returned fire. A yelp behind him told Luke the soldier was now playing for keeps. When he looked back, he saw a security guard had been hit in the chest plate and knocked off his feet. Now the man was scrambling back for the doorway.

With the complex mainframe down, the rules had changed. There was no more letting them go. Rounds peppered around Luke's feet, and the back window of the Suburban exploded. Luke ran past Weaver, who was firing rapidly, suppressing the SWAT team members trying to get out the door.

Luke slapped the quarter panel of the SUV then turned and fired, allowing Weaver to peel back. As soon as he let up, the security team leaned out of the garage and fired blind on them. He slapped the Suburban with his left hand again. "Go, go, go, get back to the Beast; we'll cover you."

He dropped to a knee and bled off an entire magazine, aiming low, letting rounds skip off the gravel, peppering the entrance with stones and dust. Weaver was up and running past him several yards before dropping and doing the same, saying, "We're going to have to start killing these guys. They seem awful pissed off."

They bounded back, taking turns suppressing the door until they'd reached a tree line. A man burst from the entry, his rifle in the shoulder, firing indiscriminately in the wrong direction. Going from the dark room and into the bright sunlight provided momentary blindness that Luke and Weaver took advantage of.

Luke clenched his teeth, not wanting to do it. He aimed low at the man's shins and fired three rounds, the third hitting just above the ankle, in an armored shin plate. The man tumbled in the air like he'd been blasted by a Louisville Slugger, screaming in agony, the leg probably broken.

"They probably think we took the whole place down," Luke said frantically, scrambling for a reload.

Weaver was back up, watching the door. Every time a man stepped out, he would place accurate fire all over him. "We didn't?"

"No time to tell you the details, but no."

Luke looked around. He could see the large radio tower to their southwest. Pointing it out to Weaver, he said, "Let's get the hell out of Dodge. I don't think lights are going to make a difference to them." Together, they emptied another magazine then spun back into the tree line and took off at a full sprint.

They found they were running downhill, scrambling between trees. The duo crossed over an open street and into another tree line on the other side. The pair stopped and leaned against trees, panting, while they reloaded their weapons and listened for anyone pursuing them. After a short pause, Luke looked at his watch. "Power has to be back up by now. Maybe they figured out this fight ain't worth it."

Weaver looked at him and shook his head.

"Brother, I am so damn confused right now. What exactly did you do?"

"That doctor gave me some tool, something on a thumb drive. It forced a reboot to their central mainframe then hosed up whatever was causing the jamming."

Pushing a finger in and out of his closed fist, Weaver grinned. "Damn Casanova, I don't know how you do it."

Luke shook his head at the soldier. "You know you all have problems, right?" He stepped back into the road, spun a quick 360, then pointed. "It's this way."

Weaver nodded and followed him. "So this program, it only broke the jamming?"

"That's what she said." Luke stopped and looked down the road. The MRAP was on the move and headed in their direction with the Suburban just behind it. "Now who in the hell is driving my truck?"

He stepped off to the side and waited as the MRAP rolled past them then stopped. The door opened with Tucker in the driver's seat. Luke began to chew him out, when the man reached to the center and flipped on the radio.

Luke smiled, hearing radio traffic. It was a HAM radio operator in Maryland. Tucker turned the knob and they heard another. Nearly every frequency had people talking.

The jammer was down.

CHAPTER TWENTY-FOUR

DAY OF INFECTION, PLUS TWENTY

Near Hayslette, Virginia

The big rig pulled to the shoulder of the road and cut the engine. Joe jumped from the driver's door and ran to a nearby bush, dropping his pants and squatting. Men lining the top of the box trailer slid down ropes to the ground and unlatched the rear doors. They were parked on a high overlook, a hilltop with wide grassy plains that showed no signs of life, but more importantly, no Primals. In the distance, just short of the horizon, they could see Camp Alamo. The camp was in a fight for its life, surrounded with Marines firing into the hordes pressed up against the walls.

Mega pulled himself through a hole in the roof and walked toward the cab of the truck.

"Why are we stopping?" a man asked.

Pointing at the battle in the valley below them,

Mega said, "That's where we're headed. You really want to go there right now?"

The man looked at the battle, his brow tightened.

"Yeah, I didn't think so," Mega scoffed. "Just be happy we finally stopped. Go drink some water and change your socks."

"Do what?" the man said, confused.

"Stop bothering me," Mega barked, causing the man to flinch so hard he nearly fell off the trailer.

The soldier was tired and dirty, having spent the entire day and night loading survivors and then trying to fight back Primals as they navigated the big truck down county roads. His armor was covered in blood and sweat, and earlier he'd stepped in something in the trailer that he didn't even want to know what it was.

He was done with all of it, and just a little pissed at Gyles for not rotating him into the cab for at least a tiny bit of sleep. He grabbed a rope at the front of the box trailer and slid down to the ground. He saw Kenny and Culver gathered off to the right in the high grass. They were standing with cigarettes dangling from their lips, watching the distant battle.

"Hey, dickwads. I ain't riding in that trailer anymore. One of you fools needs to switch with me."

Kenny shook his head. "Not me, Hoss, I'm the navigator."

Culver frowned. "No can do, buddy. I'm keeping Joe straight... who knows what he might do if I leave him alone."

"Screw that noise, I ain't riding in the trailer

anymore." He turned and looked toward the cab. "Hey, where's Sergeant Gyles?"

Culver looked down and moved his head side to side. "Not here."

"What the hell is that supposed to mean?" Mega said, his chest puffing out, his temper beginning to rage. "Where is he?"

Kenny took a step toward the big man. "I'm sorry, Mega. Sergeant Gyles didn't get on the truck."

"Nahh... bullshit. I saw him jump onto the garage to help with evacuations. He made it across, I saw him. We got everyone out, even that priest and his boyfriend." The big man walked to the cab of the truck and climbed up, looking into the sleeper cab. He looked back at the soldiers. "Where is he?"

Culver swallowed hard. "He's with the Hummer. He went ahead to clear a path. He's probably down there at Camp Alamo right now."

Mega put his head back and wiped his brow with his forearm. "Holy hell, you guys scared the shit out of me. Why you guys always messing with me? Shit ain't funny."

A large explosion in the distance turned them around. A fireball hundreds of yards long erupted in front of Alamo's walls. In the air, a pair of F35s screamed by in a long arc then came back for a second napalm run.

Kenny pointed. "Those are zoomies! The Air Force is back!"

EPILOGUE

Taking the water jug, Gyles spun off the cap and tried to pour it over his head, getting a small stream of warm water for his efforts. He kicked at the door, it finally breaking free on the third blast from his boot. The steel door swung open with a shrill screech. He tried to step out but mostly fell then rolled to the ground, landing on the scorched remains of a body. He pushed up and pressed back against the Humvee. The street was destroyed, lined with burnt-out cars and the smoldering bodies of the dead, the buildings nothing but smoking rubble.

Gyles rested his head against the body of the vehicle, breathing hard. He'd passed out sometime during the night, waking at every scream and moan of the infected as they walked the streets, despite the blazing flames. He heard every explosion in the burning city, felt the rumble of every collapse. Somehow, his vehicle in the intersection survived the devastation, even if it nearly roasted him alive. Near his boots was a naked body, its skin blackened, the hair burnt away. The damn things followed him here. Even burning to death, they followed him.

Taking a deep breath, he forced himself to his knees and then up to his feet. He walked back to the door and reached into his pack, grabbing a half full canteen. He spun the cap and drank until it was gone. Then he stepped back and looked at the Humvee. It was completely pinned in by the steel pole, two of its tires flat. No way he was getting it free. He reached inside, grabbed his poncho liner, and stuffed it back into his pack. He looked at his armor and shook his head, deciding to leave it.

He turned and began walking down the center of the street toward the church. His mind was dulled, his thoughts clouded. Looking left and right, there were no people, no infected. Everything was ash, everything destroyed. His skin was pelted with black snow falling from the sky, the only thing that remained of the city. He laughed for a second, then choked on the smoke. "I did this; I burnt you down," he said, looking at buildings.

In the smoky haze of the skyline, he could just make out the church tower. He stood motionless, blinking away the sting in his eyes. As the smoke cleared, he could see that the tower was different. The top portion of the bell platform had collapsed. He stopped and turned around, everything destroyed. He had nowhere to go.

The sound of car engines replaced the silence that had overtaken the city. Ahead of him, he could see their outlines—a convoy of black SUVs. They drove right toward him, not slowing down. He held his ground, not out of defiance, but out of shock. With only feet to spare, the lead vehicle hit the brakes. Doors opened and men in black utility uniforms spread out, covering the street.

A man stepped from the passenger side of the lead vehicle. The stranger was wearing black cargo pants, with a black shirt and black combat boots. The only part of the man's uniform that wasn't black was the T-shirt he wore under his top. It was white, its brightness reflecting at him. Gyles laughed, thinking he was imagining it all.

The man looked at Gyles and said, "What's so funny?"

"You all can relax," Gyles said. "It's safe here."

"Relax?" the man asked.

Gyles laughed again. "City is clear; I already killed them all."

The driver looked at Gyles nervously, then to the man next to him. "I think this guy has lost it."

This caused another burst of laughter from Gyles. "What business do you have in my city?"

"Are you Army? We were told all of the Army had pulled out of here," the driver said.

Nodding, Gyles grunted, "Yeah, I am the Army."

"Sergeant Gyles?" a voice shouted from the back.

A pair of men dressed in the same black uniforms

ran forward from a trail vehicle. Gyles staggered back, feeling drunk on his feet. He focused on the men. He knew who they were, but their names wouldn't register in his still spinning brain. He dropped to a knee, his rifle hitting the ground next to him with a clack. Then he fell back onto his rear, sitting in the street.

"We should leave him. He's probably infected," he heard the driver say.

Gyles looked up and tried to focus.

"No, we aren't leaving him," said one of the men whose names Gyles couldn't remember, running to his side. The man put his hands on Gyles's face. "Sergeant Gyles, it's me—Corporal Rodriguez." The medic looked back toward the line of vehicles and shouted, "Get Doctor Howard up here now! I know this man!"

THANK YOU FOR READING

Please leave a review on Amazon.

ABOUT THE AUTHOR

W. J. Lundy is a still serving Veteran of the U.S. Military with service in Afghanistan. He has over 16 years of combined service with the Army and Navy in Europe, the Balkans and Southwest Asia. W.J. is an avid athlete, writer, backpacker and shooting enthusiast. He currently resides with his wife and daughter in Central Michigan.

Join the WJ Lundy mailing list for news, updates and contest giveaways.

http://www.wjlundy.com

ALSO BY W.J. LUNDY

Whiskey Tango Foxtrot Series.

Whiskey Tango Foxtrot is an introduction into the apocalyptic world of Staff Sergeant Brad Thompson.   A series with over 1,500 five-star reviews on Amazon.

Alone in a foreign land. The radio goes quiet while on convoy in Afghanistan, a lost patrol alone in the desert. With his unit and his home base destroyed, Staff Sergeant Brad Thompson suddenly finds himself isolated and in command of a small group of men trying to survive in the Afghan wasteland.

Every turn leads to danger. The local population has been afflicted with an illness that turns them into rabid animals. They pursue him and his men at every corner and stop. Struggling to hold his team together and unite survivors, he must fight and evade his way to safety.

A fast paced zombie war story like no other.

Escaping The Dead

Tales of The Forgotten

Only The Dead Live Forever

Walking In The Shadow Of Death

Something To Fight For

Divided We Fall

Bound By Honor

Primal Resurrection

Praise for Whiskey Tango Foxtrot:

"The beginning of a fantastic story. Action packed and full of likeable characters. If you want military authenticity, look no further. You won't be sorry."

-Owen Baillie, Author of Best-selling series, Invasion of the Dead.

"A brilliantly entertaining post-apocalyptic thriller. You'll find it hard to putdown"

-Darren Wearmouth, Best-selling author of First Activation, Critical Dawn, Sixth Cycle

"W.J. Lundy captured two things I love in one novel-- military and zombies!"

-Terri King, Editor Death Throes Webzine

"War is horror and having a horror set during wartime works well in this story. Highly recommended!"

-Allen Gamboa, Author of Dead Island: Operation Zulu

THE INVASION TRILOGY

The Darkness is a fast-paced story of survival that brings the apocalypse to Main Street USA.

While the world falls apart, Jacob Anderson barricades his family behind locked doors. News reports tell of civil unrest in the streets, murders, and disappearances; citizens are warned to remain behind locked doors. When Jacob becomes witness to horrible events and the alarming actions of his neighbors, he and his family realize everything is far worse than being reported.

Every father's nightmare comes true as Jacob's normal life--and a promise to protect his family--is torn apart.

From the Best-Selling Author of **Whiskey Tango Foxtrot comes a new telling of Armageddon.**

The Darkness

The Shadows

The Light

Trilogy

Praise for the Invasion Trilogy:

"The Darkness is like an air raid siren that won't shut off; thrilling and downright horrifying!" *Nicholas Sansbury*

Smith, Best Selling Author of Orbs and The Extinction Cycle.

"Absolutely amazing. This story hooked me from the first page and didn't let up. I read the story in one sitting and now I am desperate for more. ...Mr. Lundy has definitely broken new ground with this tale of humanity, sacrifice and love of family ... In short, read this book." *William Allen, Author of Walking in the Rain.*

"First book I've pre-ordered before it was published. Well done story of survival with a relentless pace, great action, and characters I cared about! Some scenes are still in my head!" *Stephen A. North, Author of Dead Tide and The Drifter.*

DONOVAN'S WAR

The Author of the bestselling series *Whiskey Tango Foxtrot,* returns with Tommy Donovan, on a war path of destruction to save the only family he has left.

With everything around him gone. Tommy Donovan must return to the war he has been hiding from. When his sister is taken, the Government fails to act. Tommy Donovan will take the law into his own hands. But, this time he isn't a soldier, and there will be no laws to protect evil. This time it's personal and he is making the rules.

Resigned to never finding peace from the war long behind him, retired warrior, Thomas Donovan, is now faced with an even deadlier conflict... one that could cost him the last of his humanity.

Once a member of an elite underground unit, the only wars Thomas knows now are the ones that rage inside him. All he wants is to stay under the radar of existence, trying to forget the past and isolating himself from the present.

When extremists kidnap a group of women from a Christian church in Syria, the past and present collide,forcing Donovan to act. This time, the battle is personal. This time, evil has chosen the wrong victim, and Thomas Donovan will not stop until he has made those responsible pay.

Facing insurmountable odds in hostile territories and always one step behind, will he be too late to save the life of the one he holds dear?

"Riveting unexpected twists, gritty realism, and first-hand adventure are inside this book. Get it now." - *JL Bourne, author of Tomorrow War and Day by Day Armageddon.*

"Donovan's War is an intense, non-stop thriller that begins with just enough of the main character's back-story to make you want to keep reading, without getting you bogged down with page after page of info dump to establish that Tommy is a world-class bad ass." Brian Parker, author of A Path of Ashes.

They took Tommy's Sister ...and you don't mess with Tommy's family.

Buy Now

OTHER BOOKS FROM UNDER THE
SHIELD OF

LABYRINTH ROYALE

CARL SINCLAIR

Jason Bell, pro gamer finds himself pulled inside of the dangerous video game Labyrinth Royale. Once inside he realises the rules of the game have real world implications, on his friends, world and his own life. This book is for fans of battle royales, shooting bad guys and movies like Jumanji 2.

You can pre order now on Amazon

FIVE ROADS TO TEXAS

| LUNDY | GAMBOA | HANSEN | BAKER | PARKER |

From the best story tellers of Phalanx Press comes a frightening tale of Armageddon.

It spread fast- no time to understand it- let alone learn how to fight it.

Once it reached you, it was too late. All you could do is run.

Rumored safe zones and potential for a cure drifted across the populace, forcing tough decisions to be made.

They say only the strong survive. Well they forgot about the smart, the inventive and the lucky.

Follow five different groups from across the U.S.A. as they make their way to what could be America's last stand in the Lone Star State.

GET IT NOW ON AMAZON

AFTER THE ROADS

BRIAN PARKER

The infected rule the world beyond the protective walls of the Texas Safe Zone.

Fort Bliss, Texas is home to four million refugees, trapped behind the hastily-erected walls of the Army base--too many people and not enough food.

In a desperate gamble, the soldiers responsible for securing the walls begin searching for pre-outbreak food storage locations. Not everyone will make it home.

For Sidney Bannister, the Safe Zone's refugee camps have become a nightmare that she can no longer endure. She must find a way to leave before her baby is born, or risk never experiencing freedom again.

Follow Sidney's story from the Phalanx Press collaborative novel Five Roads to Texas.

FOR WHICH WE STAND

JOSEPH HANSEN

El Paso wasn't the Promised Land that Ian and his crew had hoped for but it wasn't a total bust either. The concept of a safe haven in today's world was a fool's errand at best. This was the consensus of their tiny band and to keep moving, their only salvation. While others waited in their pens the four from the private security company moved on taking on as many they could help, in hopes that they too would join the fight. Their journey was long and arduous but it was worth it... they hope.

El Paso is where the final evidence that this is more than a simple lab experiment gone wrong. It was too focused with too many players who knew too much too early in the game causing assumptions to be made. Assumptions that gained strength with every step they took until the small troop was convinced that this was not just a simple virus of natural origins, America was under attack.

For Which We Stand is a post-apocalyptic thriller that lends credence to the fears that many share. Is it possible? No one can say, Five Roads to Texas is but one of hundreds end of the world scenarios. We all know it's coming, how and when is the only question.

CONVERGENCE

AJ POWERS

Even in death, life rarely goes as planned.

Having nothing left to live for, Malcom is given a shot at redemption when a woman named Tessa needs his help. With death looming, Malcom, Tessa and her children flee Cincinnati with their sights set on El Paso. They know the trip won't be easy, but nothing could prepare them for the nightmares ahead.

Follow these new characters in the Five Roads to Texas series as they set sail on a harrowing journey to what might be the last bastion of hope in America.

Book 4 in the Five Roads to Texas series

SHOWDOWN AT CHIMNEY ROCK

RICH BAKER

A global pandemic burns through the population leaving America in shambles.

Sarah Washburn and her crew are forced to go on the run from an indefensible horde.

Isolated in the Colorado high country, they're pursued at every turn by mercenaries who want something they have.

An impossible situation with low odds of survival, and their luck running out, they have one shot.

A final chance to take a stand in a showdown that will alter the fate of the new world.

DEAD ISLAND: OPERATION ZULU

ALLEN GAMBOA

Ten years after the world was nearly brought to its knees by a zombie Armageddon, there is a race for the antidote! On a remote Caribbean island, surrounded by a horde of hungry living dead, a team of American and Australian commandos must rescue the Antidotes' scientist. Filled with zombies, guns, Russian bad guys, shady government types, serial killers and elevator muzak. Dead Island is an action packed blood soaked horror adventure.

INVASION OF THE DEAD SERIES

OWEN BALLIE

This is the first book in a series of nine, about an ordinary bunch of friends, and their plight to survive an apocalypse in Australia. -- Deep beneath defense headquarters in the Australian Capital Territory, the last ranking Army chief and a brilliant scientist struggle with answers to the collapse of the world, and the aftermath of an unprecedented virus. Is it a natural mutation, or does the infection contain -- more sinister roots? -- One hundred and fifty miles away, five friends returning from a month-long camping trip slowly discover that death has swept through the country. What greets them in a gradual revelation is an enemy beyond compare. -- Armed with dwindling ammunition, the friends must overcome their disagreements, utilize their individual skills, and face unimaginable horrors as they battle to reach their hometown...

THIS BOOK WAS FORMATTED BY

CARLSINCLAIR.NET

Made in the USA
Las Vegas, NV
03 May 2024

89485828R00184